SICKER B*STARDS

MATT SHAW

Sick B*stards II

CHAPTER 1

Haunted Memories

The sight of the skin being pulled from the writhing body made our mouths water. Each of us, in turn, licked our lips with Sister licking her lips in such a way my excitement could only grow. I wasn't sure whether I wanted her more, or the meat which was to follow. Both tasted just as good as the other. As Father continued to stretch skin away from muscle my thoughts drifted to the possibility of mixing the two succulent flavours; cunt and flesh. Two of my five a day. Specifically my memories pulled up old sex games my friends told me of, when I was growing up (if my damaged memory serves me correctly). Mars Bar Parties. A chocolate bar would be inserted into a lady's vagina before being eaten back out - no hands permitted. In my darkened thoughts I was imagining a similar game but one which saw the chocolate bar replaced with slithers of still warm skin to lap out of the girl's moist pussy. I felt myself harden at the thought as I wondered whether Sister would be up for it too?

"What's wrong with you?" Sister asked. She was staring directly at me and I hadn't noticed - so wrapped up in my own demented little world with a wry smile spread across my face.

I couldn't help but laugh, "Nothing," I said, too ashamed to admit to my family what was going through my mind. Not sure why really. The things we've seen and done, since being trapped in this house...Nothing should shock us anymore. Hell, for all I know, Mother and Father may want to try my little party game out too (or have already done so).

Father started dishing out the various pieces of skin onto our waiting plates. At the first opportunity, when no one was looking, I pocketed one of the smaller pieces he'd dropped onto my own plate as the thought of eating it from my Sister's sweetness continued to excite me. Tonight is the night.

I had hurried through my meat as fast as I possibly could. Unlike my earlier days of eating it, where I wanted to just get through it quickly before I realised what I was eating, nowadays I tended to enjoy it that little bit more and really take my time. Something to do with accepting where I was, I guess. This is me. This is who I am. This is my life now. Not today though. Today I wanted it eaten quickly so I could get upstairs and eat the slither (which was festering away in my pocket) from my sister as my tainted imagination instructed.

By the time we both got to the bedroom, and closed the door behind us, we were already stripping off each other's clothes. I remember a time when there was a feeling of guilt mixed within the lustful thoughts but those days are gone. Now it's all about the lust. The wanting. The need. I pushed her back onto the mattress when she was down to bra and panties. She landed with a smile on her face and a naughty twinkle in her eyes. She drives me wild.

"Want to try something?" I asked her.

Her smile broadened. "What is it?" she asked.

"Lie back and close your eyes."

She didn't need telling twice. I reached to my trousers and pulled out the piece of meat I had stolen from downstairs. A smile on my face as I wrapped it around two of my fingers on my left hand. I cast my eyes back to Sister. Her head was tilted back, her eyes were shut - expectation of a new sensation clear on her face. I positioned myself above her. She opened her legs to allow me access to her sweet, sweet pussy.

"Ready?"

She giggled unaware of what was coming next. I couldn't help but laugh too as I pushed my fingers (and the meat) inside of her. Immediately she could tell it wasn't just my fingers and she questioned my actions, "What is that?" I didn't answer. I continued to thrust in and out of her (pulling the meat out and pushing it back in again) instead before I could take no more and had to taste it. I continued to thrust as I re-positioned myself and then, when my head was between her legs, I withdrew my two sopping fingers and replaced them with my tongue. Delicious. The fishy taste of an unwashed vagina (just the way I like it now I've grown accustomed to it) mixed with the irony taste of the drying blood upon the meat...And not forgetting the tastes of the meat itself. An explosion of tastes and experiences upon my tongue. Heaven. I looked up to her face to see if she was enjoying the sensation and noticed she was looking at me. Her eyes filled with lust. She could see what I was using as a new sex toy. "Kiss me," she ordered. I didn't need asking twice. With the meat gripped in my mouth I pulled away leaving it hanging from mouth to chin. I moved up her body until we were face to face with the meat dangling above her own mouth. Within seconds she had the other end between her teeth as I snowballed it across to her - sucking and chewing upon it as our heads moved closer together like a crazy scene from the Disney cartoon *Lady and the Tramp*. As we passed the meat from my mouth to hers and back again, I couldn't help but wonder whether we were both sharing the taste or fighting over it. I felt her hand wrap around my penis as she guided me into her sopping pussy - wet from my saliva and her own natural juices. I slid in easily, with a sigh "Fuck me!" she ordered.

I released my end of the meat to concentrate on the fucking. It dropped from my mouth but it wasn't wasted. She caught it and started chewing - her eyes locked onto mine. I didn't think it possible but I felt myself harden more so than I had done before; the sight of her eating the flesh, the lust in her eyes, the tightness of her cunt. And to think - I ran away from this. I didn't want a part of it. A moment of madness. I live for this. I want this. This is who I am. This is who we are.

I felt the stirrings of a powerful orgasm and increased my rhythm.

⅄

A New Day

I woke up with a start. A sickness brewing in my stomach as the nightmare continued to haunt me despite being awake. Usually forget dreams pretty fast, when

I wake, but not this time - can't seem to shake it. It's one thing living like this because I don't have an alternative option but it doesn't mean I have to enjoy it. I *won't* enjoy it. At least not to *that* kind of level. I sat up on the stained mattress and turned to look at my sister...My *sister*? Not my sister... I've been back here for a couple of days now and the damned water - drugged with whatever the government people were lacing it with - still hasn't blocked out the recovered memories I'd sooner forget. I thought it would have. Drank a pint of the damned stuff as soon as I set foot back inside the house and awoke with not only my recently recovered memories plaguing me but also a headache. Now, when I sit with my *family* I can't help but feel jealous of their ignorance in the truth of our situation; stuck out here as a fucked up experiment designed to satisfy the twisted minds of the curious. I look at them sitting around the house living in a blissful ignorance and I'm jealous but at the same time part of me feels conflicted and I pity them for not knowing the real reason we're living as we are and that, just a few miles from where we're feasting upon left over flesh which is definitely past its best, civilisation continues to go on just as it had always done. They move on. We sink further into the cesspit. Sister stirred and opened her eyes. She saw me looking at her and smiled. *That* smile.

"Morning," she sighed. She reached up to where I was sitting and put her arms around me, dragging me back until I was lying next to her. "I'm glad you came home," she said, "I missed you." I ignored the images of her fucking father flickering through my mind. I hadn't been out of the house for very long at all and yet there she was, clearly visible on one of the cabin's monitors...With him. She missed me so much she jumped into bed with the man she believed to be her father.

This whole situation is a mess. One minute I think I'm okay with it and the next I find myself contemplating telling her. Not just her. Them. I see myself telling *them* what's happened. There was no nuke. Civilisation didn't die. We aren't the last few left and the *things* roaming the woods outside aren't infected by some kind of radiation - at least not from a bomb. They're infected okay, with whatever it is the scientists pumped into them.

"You're quiet," Sister said. Should speak to her. At least wish her a good morning too but it's hard to know what to say without blurting everything out - some kind of uncontrollable verbal diarrhoea.

"Just woken up," I lied, "brain isn't working yet..."

"What about him? Is he working yet?" she reached down, still smiling, and groped at my penis. With her touch, and despite my poisoned thoughts, it didn't take long for *him* to stand to attention. I'm thankful. Not for her touch (as lovely as it is) but for my erection. Given all we've been through together, mostly in this room, a flaccid penis could have raised some questions. Sister changed position, forcing me onto my back, before she went down on me. The first I felt, other than her hand which was still on my shaft, was a flick of her tongue. Usually I'd just lie there and enjoy the feelings but today was harder - I couldn't help but wonder where the cameras were hidden in this room. The cameras they used to spy on us, to see how we'd react to our situation. Not hard to see how we didn't find the cameras - even knowing it's in the room, I still can't see it. Or them.

Sister's other hand cupped my balls. A gentle squeeze which gradually got harder as the intensity of her mouth and hand action (on my shaft) increased. Yet I still can't focus on the pleasures. Not properly. Not knowing someone could be watching us. I wonder whether, with their beady eyes on us, they wanked their cocks as we put a show on for them. Maybe they took turns pleasuring each other? *You do me, I'll do you.* Not just men in there watching either - maybe some women were flicking themselves along to our hardcore show...Well...They want a show...Whoever may or may not be watching We'll give them a fucking show.

I pulled away from Sister.

"What's wrong?" she asked as she licked her lips.

"Turn round," I instructed her. She did as she was told and faced away from me on her hands and knees - arse in the air. I looked towards the far side of the room, where I presumed the cameras to be, and gave them a wink before turning my attention back to Sister. Without a second thought to the potential viewers I bent down, ripped her underwear off and stuck my tongue deep in her arsehole. A shocked noise escaped her mouth (followed by a sigh as I pushed my tongue in deeper). Not surprising really. This is definitely a first. And not because I had a sudden urge to taste her but because I knew it would need some kind of lubrication and, when lube is in short supply, spit'll do. I wiped my thumb in the spit which ran down the crack of Sister's pert arse and pushed it, gently, against the inviting hole. She breathed in followed by an expectant sigh. I pushed in until I was knuckle deep. Sister, to my surprise, pushed back and gave a slight wiggle as though enjoying the sensation. I couldn't help but wonder whether this was something she'd been used to in the real world before we were placed here. Slowly, at first, she started bouncing back against my thumb - almost fucking herself with it. I stayed still. Let her do the work (for now) whilst I enjoyed the tempting view. I dribbled more spit onto my thumb again before it disappeared back into her arse. A few more bounces, by Sister, and I withdrew it. Clean, thankfully. I lined the throbbing head of my penis against the orifice and hesitated a moment, unsure whether she'd be as willing. After all - a bit of a size difference between thumb and erection.

"Do it!" she ordered. She pushed back as I pushed forward. It slipped inside easier than I'd have thought it would have. No doubt helped by the spit and the loosening (thanks to the thumb). As the tight hole swallowed the length of my shaft we both gasped out loud. The tightness strangling my penis being a great sensation for me. The thick shaft stretching her open causing her to lose her breath. "Go slow!" she whispered. I could tell by the tone in her voice it was stinging her. I didn't care, though. Those fucks - out there in the cabins - watching...They like to watch. I'll give them a show. I moved my hips back, mostly pulling my penis from her arse, before thrusting forward hard. Sister screamed out loud. I'll take that as a scream of ecstasy. I pulled back before thrusting forward again. Another great sensation and another scream; both of which simply enticed me to continue but with added speed. Soon I was pumping hard, with my hands on either cheek, and her screams had turned to low grunts. More than that - it wasn't long before she was thrusting herself back against my penis like a woman who couldn't get enough of the feeling of being filled. Perhaps helped by the fact I realised she was rubbing her clit with her left hand whilst her right hand stayed firmly on the mattress in order to stop us from falling face first onto the mattress in a dirty, incestuous heap. Not incest. Not my sister. "Harder!" she begged me. "Fuck me harder!" Guess her arse has got used to the thickness of my cock and the deepness of my thrusts. I increased speed as I turned towards the wall - still trying to remember where the camera position had been filmed from and curious as to whether there'd be anyone watching us now; perhaps some lone survivor hiding away, like Michael Bray had been when I found him cowering under his desk, or maybe new recruits who'd been sent down to clean the mess up.

I felt the familiar build up of what seemed to be an intense orgasm; helped by Sister's newfound trick of repeatedly clenching her arse cheeks around me as I continued to thrust. A tingling sensation in the thighs, then in the testicles and then twitch after twitch from my penis as my semen filled her arse. Couldn't remain quiet as I grunted out loud. As soon as I'd finished ejaculating, I couldn't help but to collapse on Sister who buckled under my sudden weight. I pulled back allowing my penis to slop out in a sticky mess of white and brown.

"Have I shit myself?" Sister asked. A worried tone in her voice. Who said romance was dead? "Fuck me that was intense," she laughed. I didn't respond. I wasn't being rude. It's just - by the time my brain had figured out what she'd said - it was too late. No point in filling the silence between us. Besides which I was still staring dead ahead at the wall. As soon as Sister goes to the bathroom to sort herself out (as was common practice after a fuck), I'd have a closer look at the wall. See if I can find that camera. Rip it from the wall. Even if the cabins are still full of dead scientists and their ghosts - I'm not comfortable with the possibility of someone watching whenever they felt like it. Funny really considering the show I'd just put on. I hope someone was there to enjoy it because it was the last they'd get to see.

Sister pulled her knickers up. A glimpse of her rear, as she did so, suggested it was for the best as I could clearly see her backside was starting to cream-pie with my juices.

"I'll be back in a minute," she said. And with that she disappeared from the room. Immediately I jumped up, not even bothering to pull my own boxers up, and hurried over to the wall. I started by looking at the top corners but I couldn't see anything. No holes. No obvious hiding place for a camera.

"Come on, where are you?" I asked as though the camera were suddenly going to be able to answer me back. *I'm over here.* Stupid. I turned my attention to the desk on the table. Various items lying on top of it - paper, photographs of the people who had once lived here (did anyone live here or is it just a set?) and the odd book. A cluttered mess not unlike the kind you'd find in my own home. Thinking back to the view I saw, of the room, back in the cabin - there's a strong possibility that the camera

7

would be somewhere amongst this lot. Hidden in the debris of someone's lost life. But where? A glance over the varied items doesn't reveal any hidden wires or of anything noteworthy. Are they really that small that they're nearly impossible to see? Why am I surprised? They'd hardly be of any use if they were the size of a standard camera. Not when it comes to spying on people, such as my family (not my family dammit). Without any thought to the noise it'd make, I gave a giant sweep of my right arm - sending everything on the desk crashing to the floor. If it were amongst the items littered across the wooden top then it certainly wouldn't be there now.

"What are you doing?" Sister asked from the doorway.

I span around. She was standing there, a look of bemusement on her face.

"Getting it ready for later," I said - thinking on my feet. "Haven't fucked on it yet." I flashed her a smile, hoping she'd buy my quick lie.

She smiled back, "You honestly think it would take the weight?"

She bought it.

"Be fun to find out," I told her.

She walked towards me and grabbed a hold of my semi-erect penis, ignoring the sticky state our latest escapades had left it in, "Think you could go again so soon?"

"Not interrupting am I?" Mother spoke from the doorway, a look of jealousy on her face similar to the look I'd seen on Sister's when she'd seen Mother and I closer than we should have been. Sister didn't pull away. She just flashed her a smile. Perhaps a silent (smug) way to say that I was with her and there was nothing she could do about it. "Father wants a meeting downstairs," she said. She hesitated for a moment, maybe waiting for us to say 'okay' or something similar, before she stepped from the room (leaving the door open as she did so).

Sister turned to me, the same smile on her face, "To be continued!"

I smiled back at her just to keep her happy. The more I thought about it, the more I couldn't help but think I was better off taking my own life. Pity I was too chicken shit. I can't go back to the real world, I understand that, but I'm not sure I can live like this either.

Sister hurried across the room to where her clothes had been thrown on the floor the previous night. She started to put them on and I did the same with my own clothes. Best not keep Father waiting.

⅄

A Family Meeting

"Still here then," Father mocked me as I walked into the dining room where he was sitting. I didn't bother answering him back. There was no point in making him angry. I should just be thankful he let me back into the house in the first place. Can't rock the boat now. Now I know, for a fact, that there is nowhere out there for me. For us. "Sit!" he ordered us.

I walked in and sat down in my usual seat. Sister sat opposite me, still smiling. You could see, in her eyes, that she was still hungry for more of what she'd received this morning. Insatiable. Hadn't seen her like that before. Clearly a fan of the kinkier side of life.

"Where's Mother?" I asked Father in an effort to distract myself from the fresh images of Sister's arse being penetrated by my penis. On cue Mother walked into the room with a tray. On that tray were four cups of water. Pints no less. The first *breakfast* for a while now where there hadn't been any meat waiting on the table for us. Mother put the cups down and took her seat next to me. Her hand under the table gave my leg a little squeeze. I turned to her curious to see what she was doing. She wasn't paying me any attention. She was simply staring ahead at Sister. A smile on her face which mirrored the smile Sister had given her earlier in the bedroom. Great. Piggy in the middle.

"The good news," Father said, his voice breaking the sudden awkwardness I was feeling, "is that the water still works and it's plentiful. The bad news is that the same can't be said for food." Hardly surprising the *food* is starting to run out - considering the state the 'facility' was in, on the other side of the fence. "I think it's fair to say," Father continued, "that you may have been right about the lack of help coming," he was looking directly at me, "and that we could well be alone...With the exception of those *things* out there..." I squirmed on my seat. I didn't like where this was headed. "I checked the car you brought back - there's a little fuel left. Now we have a choice..." and here it is, "we can stay here, as originally intended, or we can go out and see if we can find somewhere else...Somewhere with food - maybe even some survivors." I knew I shouldn't have come home in the car. I knew I should have parked it up somewhere out of sight. The temptation for Father to take us away from here and towards the uncomfortable truth of what really happened to force us into this godforsaken nightmare in the first place. Can't let this happen.

"I've seen what's out there waiting for us," I butted in with my opinion before anybody had a chance to go with his idea of leaving the house, "and there's nothing out there for us. At least here we have sanctuary."

"And the possibility of starvation." Father argued. It was clear from the look on his face that he'd already made the decision for us. He wanted to take the car and drive off to whatever he believed was out there waiting for him (us). I'm not entirely sure where the sudden change of mind had come from. Before I had left to see what was out there, he had been adamant that staying in the house - and waiting - was the best decision. Now it feels as though he can't get out fast enough. A small part of my mind wondering whether the sudden turnaround in thought process is because he doesn't believe what I said - when I told him there was nothing out there for us. Maybe he wants to try and prove me wrong just as I proved him wrong when he said someone would be coming for us? "It's because you've seen what is out there, or to be more precise what isn't out there, that we need to move on from here. If there really is nothing out there, just as you stated, then we will die here."

"There's a forest out there...." I went to argue.

"With those things running around it," he countered before I had a chance to finish my sentence.

A quick lie, "You think they're confined to the forests? They're not. They're everywhere. If anything - there are less in the forest than in the nearby town." I continued before he had a chance to say anything back, "We can stay here - live off what we find in the forest whether it be animals or even berries we find growing on bushes. We have more chance of staying alive if we stick to your original plan: Wait here and see who comes to find us."

"You said it yourself there's nothing out there for us," Mother said - clearly her mind was swaying towards the same thought process as Father's damaged mind. I could tell them the truth about what I had found out there. I could tell them that we're nothing but a fucked up government experiment; designed to satisfy the curious minds of the sick bastards who dreamt it up. A big game of 'what if'. What if the end of the world happened? What if people were stranded? How would they react to the situation? What if we threw this into the mix? What if....What if...I could tell them but then how'd they react? There's no way back to a normal life for us. There's no way to reverse the damage of what's happened out there. We're changed for the worse and we're stuck like this until the day we die. At least here they can live their life in what they believe to be a normal way. If I let them out there - not only will they be suffering like I am but it can only end badly. Not just for us either. For people who may happen to have the misfortune to bump into us or cross our paths. Once a killer always a killer, right?

"You're wrong anyway," Father said. I turned to him. "Something is out there. You just didn't find it."

"I saw enough..."

"Something is out there. Someone. Survivors. Otherwise - who else is flying the planes we see?" Father raised an eyebrow. I hesitated for a moment. Planes were proof enough that someone was out there - whether it be the military or pilots who've just taken a plane to get them out of the danger zone. Someone was out there. How'd he react if he knew that, chances are, they were actually commercial flights? Most likely some happy family off on their holiday; somewhere exotic with beautiful sunshine and white sandy beaches and not a care in the world other than which of the all-inclusive restaurants they should masticate in tonight.

After the hesitation I responded, "Then they'll find us."

"We are a family," Father said in a tone which revealed his irritation towards me for all to notice, "so we will put it to the vote. If you want to leave and see what we can find out there - raise your hands..." Father raised his hand before he'd even finished speaking. A second later Mother put her hand in the air too. No doubt the two of them had discussed this plan before bringing it to the table anyway. Wouldn't surprise me. Father turned to Sister - a disapproving look etched on his weary face. He (and Mother) put their hands down. "And if you want to stay here for a while longer and possibly starve to death in the process?" I raised my hand, as did Sister. I smiled at her and she smiled back. I wonder whether she even wants to stay or is just keeping me happy? "Okay - well as the head of the family - I get final say in the event of a draw and I say we leave. Today."

"What? No. Not a fucking chance!" I spat back. "We give it a couple of days, two days, and then we cast the vote again depending on whether opinions have changed. That's the fair way of doing it."

"He's right," Sister finally piped up. "What harm will two days do?"

Father sat there a moment in silence whilst grinding his teeth. "Fine!" he hissed. Without any further words he got up and left the room. Mother got up and followed - no doubt going to offer her cunt as a way of softening Father's darkened mood. I turned to Sister and smiled at her again; letting her know that, despite the foul mood of our parents (yeah right) I was there for her (just as, I presumed, she was for me). She smiled back again as my mind turned to thoughts of Father (and the way his mood was so quick to sour). I wondered whether I was protecting them from the reality of what really happened to us or whether I was protecting the outside world from us. The more I think about it, really think about it, the more I can't help but think it's more to do with the latter. It's not that I'm worried about us going back to society. I'm worried that we'll do more damage. I'm worried that we'll kill, or hurt, more people unnecessarily and then - just as Father's mood was quick to darken - so was mine as thoughts reared their ugly head in the forefront of my mind. Thoughts which hinted at the distinct possibility of having to kill my make believe family. Maybe that's the only way forward. Kill them and pluck up the courage to take my own life. Put us all out of our misery. A cold shudder rushed down my spine at the mere thought of suicide. The same reaction I've had before when my damaged mind drifted towards taking my own life. Funny how people consider those who commit suicide to be cowards. I don't. They're the brave ones. They're the ones who are able to stand up and say enough is enough. They're the ones who're able to do something about the hatred they feel for their own lives. I'm envious of them.

I was pulled from my dark thoughts by a hand rubbing my groin. I shook the thoughts off and looked down to notice Sister's hand on the crotch of my jeans. She was still smiling at me, "So - do you think you can go for a second run?" she purred. Insatiable.

CHAPTER 2

BEFORE

The Interview

I was sitting opposite the pretty technician lady who'd come and fetched me from the dismal waiting room (seriously - would it have hurt them to put some current magazines out for us to read whilst waiting...Maybe).

"We're going to ask you to confirm some details before we continue, if that's okay."

"Sure."

"Can you confirm your name?"

"John Burley." I flashed her a smile but she paid it no attention.

"And your date of birth?" she asked.

"September 30th, 1980."

"Mother's maiden name?"

"Osborne."

"Thank you. Can you confirm why you're here?"

"I was hoping you could tell me. I'm just replying to an advert."

"Can you confirm the advert and where you saw it?"

"I saw it online. It mentioned a series of scientific tests but not a lot else. Other than a substantial payment for those who completed it." I laughed. Driven by money and nothing else. I wasn't always like this but recent bills (and sudden unemployment) forced my hand. The way it stands, waiting for benefits, I'm not sure I'll ever be able to pay the debts back that I owe but this - this advert - if I complete these tests...I can pay them back in one. No more phone calls from debt collectors, no more stress, no more worry. Just a clean slate. Show me where I sign!

"There are a few forms to fill in and a few interviews to go through but the whole process should move fairly swiftly," the lady continued, "we're hoping to make our decisions as to who progresses by the end of the day."

"That's great!" I smiled. "The sooner, the better as far as I'm concerned." My heart was pounding heavily. Interviews have never been my strong point - even when I've had a chance to swat up on the subject matter I was being interviewed for. Somehow I've always managed to get it so very, very wrong. Usually by filling in the awkward silences with mindless dribble.

Lost many a job opportunity because of that. They ask you to give an example of a time you worked well in a team. You gave them an example. They just sit there and look at you as though they're waiting for you to say something else so - to avoid disappointing them - you spout out more examples with each one getting progressively worse. Not all interviews are like that though. In some I don't say enough. I give a quick example, without giving it much thought, and the interviewer nods and goes straight to the next question. By the time they've finished asking it you find you've remembered a better example. You can't back-track though. You just need to keep answering their questions as you know - deep down - it would be worse to back-track to the previous question. Yep. I hate interviews.

"Tell us about your strengths?" she asked. She opened up a clipboard, on her lap, and poised her pen ready to take some notes. I felt my heart sink. These are the questions I hate. Normally you're able to cheat. Say something you think they want to hear but when you don't even know what you're going interviewed for - it's hard to guess as to a correct answer.

"I'm a team player," I told her. "I enjoy interacting with others and pushing forward with suggestions. I find I work well in a group," the technician paused a moment as she held my gaze and then she started jotting down notes. Was that the right thing to say? "I don't have to be part of a team though. I mean, I enjoy it, but I'm more than capable of working on my own if the task calls for it. So, yeah, I'm good with either." She stopped writing and looking at me. There goes that sinking feeling again. Feels as though my heart is in the pit of my stomach now. I beg my brain to stop but before my pleas have finished I find that I'm yakking on again, "I'm a hard-worker too. I realise most people say that but I am. I enjoy it. Nothing worse than sitting around with nothing to do. Boredom sets in. Not that I sat around in my old job that much. Used my own initiative a lot, you know? Went off looking for things to do." I realised what I had said and tried to correct myself, "Not without telling people what I was doing though. I don't just disappear. Leave it for people to ask where I am before they start sending out the search parties. They know I'm around and working." Please shut up I kept screaming (internally) at my brain. I sank back in the seat with an overall feeling of despair. At least I made it through to this round, I thought. Some people didn't even get to this stage. In my mind I couldn't help but recall the time the job centre offered me an appointment to go through interview techniques. Sitting here now, feeling like a mug, I kind of wish I had taken them up on their offer.

"Thank you for that," the technician said as she scribbled the last of my rant onto the pad. She then proceeded to tick a series of boxes. Much to my frustration, I couldn't make out what they were for and whether it was a 'no' box or 'yes' box. My heart told me it was a 'no' box. My stupid brain told me I was in with a fighting change still. She stopped writing and looked me in the eye. Man she's pretty. Such blue eyes. I feel like I could go swimming in them. And then my mind lowered the tone by making me contemplate offering her some of the money, I'd get for completing the tests, just for a night with her. One night. One night to bed her as my mind took a further detour into ruder territory. "Tell me about your family," she asked.

"What family?" I said abruptly. I startled myself at how abrupt I actually was. I have family. I just don't tend to speak to them as much as other people may speak to their family members. More to the point - they don't tend to speak to me. The black sheep of the family.

⋏

NOW

Family matters

I was sitting in the living room with Sister. She was sitting next to me, nestled into my chest whilst I stroked her greasy hair. A comfortable silence between the two of us allowing my memories to dance their dance in my mind. I was the black sheep with my real family and here I was again - the black sheep with my new family.

"What's the matter?" Sister asked. She looked up at me. A genuine look of concern on her face. No doubt she doesn't want me rocking the boat again like I did last time, in the lead up to leaving the house. I couldn't tell her exactly what was on my mind. She had backed me up with regards to staying putt and not venturing out into the outside world but that doesn't mean she wouldn't run to Father and Mother if I said something slightly controversial - like the truth! I couldn't forget the way she had treated me before I left the house the first time; one minute she was close to me, even fucking me, and the next she was telling Father of my displeasure at being stuck in the house with them. Perhaps not those words exactly but she still told Father...

I thought on my feet, "Does it bother you?" I asked.

"Does what bother me?" she asked.

"This."

"What do you mean?"

I thought I had been pretty clear but I explained, "This. Where we are. Not knowing what happened to the world. Not remembering who you are. Does it bother you?"

She hesitated a moment, "I prefer not knowing," she said. "Why'd I want to remember who I was when it's only a life I can no longer have. At least this...This is all I have and this is all I know. It's simpler." Which is exactly why I chose to keep the truth of our situation a secret from her when I first came home. Not just from her - but from all of them. "Does it bother you?" she asked.

I didn't answer her. I pulled her back down onto my chest and continued to run my fingers through her hair. The truth bothered me. What those sick bastards did to us to get us here in the first place. But had I not known the truth - had I simply known as much as my pretend family; a bomb went off and supposedly wiped out humanity…Had I known nothing but the basics - bomb, humanity gone - then it would have bothered me. I would have wanted to know who dropped the bomb, I would have wanted to know why. I would have had so many questions and I know I'd be curious as to who I was before the end of the world.

"You overthink things," Sister said. She was right. I do. I wish I could switch off and just go along with the situation but I couldn't. This isn't a new trait either. Remembering the broken memories from before all of this - I have always been an over-thinker. "You'd probably be happier if you switched off from time to time."

"Wish I could." It would certainly be easier but the only way I'll be able to turn off is when I am dead. Something I am still too chicken to see through. I hesitated a moment and decided to push her further, "What if we weren't really family?"

Sister moved away from me as she sat up. She looked shocked that I'd even asked the question. "What?"

"You don't remember me and I don't remember you - not from before we all woke up together…"

"Because of the blast…Father said…"

"I know what Father said but what if he was wrong? What if we weren't family?" I continued tentatively.

"We are. There was a picture. How else would we have all been in the picture together?" she asked. I had an answer for her; the picture was faked. I didn't tell her though. I didn't push it further. I just went quiet. "Are you okay?" she asked. Another flash of concern on her face. I nodded. "You're being weird."

"I'm sorry. Just hungry." I pulled her close to my chest again. Not because I necessarily wanted to hold her close, I just wanted to stop her looking at me with those eyes for fear of seeing straight through me.

With no warning the door opened and Mother walked in. She was grinning from ear to ear. "Quick! Come through!" she disappeared again, expecting us to follow. Sister was first up and seemed to be just as excited as Mother. I didn't feel the same joyous excitement rushing through my body as they seemed to. I felt nervous. No doubt another ploy, by Father, to try and get us to leave the house. I know it is coming - the moment they discover the truth for themselves - I'm just not in a hurry for it to happen.

Father was waiting for us in the dining room. I stopped in the doorway when I saw what he was cuddling; a young cat (not quite a kitten) rubbing itself against his belly. "Shut the door!" he ordered us - no doubt worried that the cat might make a sudden run for it. It was purring as though happy to see us. I wondered whether it was a present from over the wall or whether it had lived over this side all of the time. "I was outside," Father said, "looking around, trying to decide the best route we should take when we leave…"

"We agreed to stay," I butted in.

Father shot me a look. He continued, "And this little guy came up to me. Started rubbing up against my leg…Friendly." Father gave it a stroke. I looked at Sister's face. She was grinning from ear to ear, just as Mother had been, but I know what's coming. I know what Father is about to do and I'm amazed they can't see it. I'm sure they think Father went out and came home with a new family pet. That's not what he has done, though. He has no intention of keeping this thing as a pet. A thought went through my mind; is this someone's pet already? I watched as Sister went over to the cat and started to stroke it. It responded, almost immediately, by purring loudly.

"I wonder what it's name is," Sister asked. I wanted to reach over to her and pull her away from what was coming but I wasn't quick enough.

"Dinner!" Father laughed. He scooped the cat up, in his large arms, and twisted its head with a sharp yank and a loud crack. Sister screamed out in shock. I can't believe, from all we have seen, that she hadn't expected that. I didn't move over to comfort her. Not with Father there. Father laughed again. "Want the honours?" he asked me. He held the lifeless corpse of the cat up to me. He meant for me to skin it - take away the fur so we could eat what was left behind. "Unless you want a little alone time with it first? Maybe give your sister a break from some of your sexual frustrations?" I shot Father a look but only because I couldn't believe what a hypocrite he was being. I'd seen him, on the cameras, with both Mother and Sister. He was just as bad as me.

"Pass me the knife," I said. He slid it across the table towards me. I picked it up and snatched the deceased cat away from him his other hand. The briefest of thoughts ran through my mind - stick the knife into him. End his miserable life right here, right now. The thought was fleeting. I turned to Sister, "You might want to leave the room," I told her. She was still crying for the dead animal. She left the room, followed by Mother. Funny - the things we've done, the things we've seen since being in this house... Yet when it comes to an animal being harmed - that's what sickens us.

Father stood up and walked over to me. He leaned in close to my ear and whispered, "Don't worry, son, I'll make sure they're okay..." He moved back slightly and smiled at me. The thought of stabbing him ran through my mind once more. Even had I not been able to resist acting upon impulse, I didn't get the chance to do so as he promptly left the room. Just me and the kitty. It was strange, I didn't feel as guilty as this when I killed that man - the one who had come into the house originally. Always was an animal person - another personality trait which has come flooding back to me.

Λ

BEFORE

A Death in the Family

I was standing at the counter of the veterinary centre with tears running down my face. My dad was with me. He wasn't crying. Not at the thought of the family pet being dead at least. He was more concerned about the bill and the various options the receptionist was running through with us for how they could dispose of our pet. It all seemed pointless, really. I knew what dad was going to choose. He was going to go for the cheapest option. He hated the pet when it was alive - having been forced to take it in after mum purchased it as a birthday present for me after the death of our last pet.

"And for that it will get its own crematorium. Its ashes will be placed into a small pine box for you to take away..."

I was looking at dad's face. I could tell he desperately wanted to ask how much it would cost just to take the cat away in a bin bag. Hell - he'd probably want to ask if he could just leave it with them to get rid of; let them chuck it in the bin out back as soon as our car pulled out of the customer car park. Dad fired me a look when the receptionist told him the cost of the next option. I could read him like an open book. He expected me to pay for this. The cat was my birthday present and - therefore - it meant I should have inherited all associated costs with regards to looking after it (and getting rid of the damned thing). As it was - I couldn't even afford to get myself to the vets without his help. No choice but to sell my car after more debts piled higher, crippling me more than ever.

"Or you can take Tinker away with you now," the receptionist suggested. I guess she had finally cottoned on to the fact my dad wasn't the most animal-friendly person.

Dad looked back to me again, "We can find a nice spot for him in the garden," he suggested. I nodded because I didn't want to cause a scene but inside I could not help but feel he was nothing more than a cheap bastard. He didn't want the pet in the garden, ruining any of his flower displays, but he wanted to spend additional money on him even less so. Saying we could bury the cat in the garden was just his way of saving face in front of the receptionist; his way of appearing more caring than he actually was. I knew the truth. Looking at the receptionist's expression - I think she did too.

In the car dad showed his true intentions when he turned to me and said, "Compost heap or bin - your choice." I didn't answer him. I'd already made my mind up to wait for him to go away on one of his many business trips before I'd give Tinker the proper burial he deserved. "When do you get your next Jobseeker's allowance?" he asked out of the blue.

"Friday."

"So when can I expect to see some of the money back for this?" he asked.

NOW

Ninth Life Gone

I laid the cat on the dining room table and held the knife to its soft fur. Thoughts of my old pet running through my mind as I tried to prepare myself for what needed to be done. I guess I could have refused to do it but then it would have meant Father killed the cat for nothing. At least this way we can eat. I took a handful of fur in my hands and pulled it away from the flesh of the animal. A few deep breaths and I stuck the knife in.

CHAPTER 3

NOW

End of the line

Sister was still visibly upset as we all sat around the dining room table. Pieces of cat still littered across the wooden top. Her feelings towards the animal did not stop her from having a taste though. The thoughts of the innocent animal killed for our benefit didn't seem to have any impact on our desire to eat.

"I went up to the woods," Father said. He licked his bloodied fingers. We all looked to Father, when he spoke. "You know what I heard? I mean other than the cat." No one answered him. We knew we wouldn't have long to wait for an answer. "I heard nothing." He paused a moment. "You know what I saw?" Again, no one replied. "I saw nothing." He picked another piece of meat up from his plate and shoved it in his mouth. We all watched him as he chewed it small enough to swallow. "Those things - those people...No sign of them..."

"It doesn't mean they're not there," I told him.

"... They've gone," he ignored me.

"Can't be sure."

"If we're to leave the house," he continued, "then now is the time."

"This is stupid," I said.

I knew from the first moment he mentioned leaving that we wouldn't have a choice but to go with him. What Father wants, Father gets.

"As head of this family..."

Oh, how I wanted to shout out that we weren't a family.

"… I've made the decision for us. We are leaving this house. We're going to take the car you so kindly brought back for us," his eyes fixed upon mine - unblinking, "and we're going to drive and drive and fucking drive until we run out of petrol…"

Bloodied knife sitting on the side. Reach for it. Grab it. Stick it in his throat. Sit back down, piece of cat in mouth. Watch as Father gargles through spittles of blood. Watch as he face plants onto the table top. Applause from Sister and Mother for it is I who have set them free.

"What - nothing to say?" he asked (me in particular).

He followed my gaze towards the bloodied knife. Splatters of blood and clumps of fur lingering on the blade. I took my eyes from the blade and looked at Father, trying my hardest to hide the feeling of hatred I had for the man. He knew what I was thinking; both towards him and with regards to what I wanted to do with the knife.

"It's not safe out there," I said.

No sense putting forward more of an argument. I knew he had already made his mind up. We would be leaving the house. We would be leaving…

"… The sooner the better," Father said. "We leave the sooner the better. Your Mother and I have already spoken and it has been agreed upon. Now you two have a choice. You're both of an age where you can make your own minds up so… Up to you. You can come or you can stay."

We sat there in silence. I wanted to let him leave. I wanted to let them both leave. The pair of them. Never see them again but the same can't be said for Sister. A quick glance in her direction and it's obvious she doesn't want to lose who she believes to be her parents. I don't want to lose Sister and - more than that - I can't leave Mother and Father to their own devices out there. There are people who deserve to die but I can't say for definite their (our) killing ways won't spread to those who do not deserve die.

"We're stronger if we stick together," I said. It seemed like a good thing to say. Something he'd buy. Something he'd say himself had I not said it first. The look on his face suggested he was disappointed. Guess I was supposed to say I was happy to hang around here - by myself. Too bad. I'm not leaving him with Sister. And I'm not leaving any of them to stumble upon the truth without me to hang around doing damage control.

"That's lovely!" Mother said, breaking the uncomfortable silence.

"Well then," Father smiled, "best start packing... Long journey ahead of us."

BEFORE

A Much Needed Break

I watched as mum and dad loaded the suitcases into the car. I was in the living room, looking out of the front facing window onto the driveway where dad always parked. They were both smiling. Both laughing. Both happy. It had been a while since I had seen them like this. Dad was usually stressed when he came home from work demanding a glass of whiskey be readied for him. Mum was... Well mum was usually just mum. She'd cook, she'd clean and that was pretty much it; the life he dictated to her.

"So what do you want to do today then?" Granddad asked from the living room doorway.

Just because mum and dad were off on holiday, it didn't mean they were taking me with them. I was fine with that. They needed their time alone. That was fair. But to leave Granddad in charge of me whilst they were gone? They didn't trust me? Probably expected me to throw some wild parties when they were gone, or something. I don't know.

"Could catch a movie at the cinema, or something?" he suggested.

"I'm sorry but I've already got plans with my friends," I lied. I didn't have anything lined up for the day. I just didn't fancy spending my free time with an old fuddy-duddy. His intentions were always good but - I don't know - I guess we just didn't have enough in common to be able to spend vast amounts of time together. Conversations usually dried up pretty fast. I liked computer games, spending time with my friends, going clubbing (and failing to pull) and writing. He fought in the war.

Dad walked into the room with mum in tow.

"Well we're just about done," he said, "car is loaded up and holiday spirit is engaged. Do you have everything you're going to need?" he asked Granddad.

Granddad nodded.

"Excellent." Dad turned to me, "Son, say goodbye to your mother..."

Mum walked over to me. Despite the smile on her face, I could see in her eyes that she wanted me to be going with them. We both knew dad could have afforded me to go had he wanted to do so. He was still trying to teach me a lesson though. Still trying to get me to learn the value of money and paying one's debts, I guess. Asshole.

"I wish you were coming too," mum said. She gave me a hug.

"Go. Have a good time. I'll be fine," I said - still wrapped in her arms. "I have Granddad! If anyone is getting a holiday, it's me!"

She pulled away. She knew I was just being polite and trying not to show my disappointment at not going with them. A holiday would be nice but - every cloud has a silver lining - at least I had two weeks without dad breathing down my neck. Two weeks peace and quiet whereby I could just relax.

I watched as mum and dad said goodbye to Granddad. Dad didn't say much to me other than to watch myself and try and get a job before they get home. I just smiled at him. No sense rocking the boat just as he steps foot outside of the front door. Granddad and I stood at the doorway as mum and dad climbed into the car and disappeared. Two weeks peace and quiet starting from now.

"Your dad has given me a list of jobs he needs doing before they get home," Granddad said.

Of course he did.

Funny how he got Granddad to tell me too. He knew I wouldn't be able to say no to him or kick up a fuss. Even when he isn't here he's nothing but a pain in the ass.

⅄

NOW

Roads Untraveled

I was sitting on the edge of the heavily stained mattress staring at the mess I had made earlier, knocking things from the table. My thoughts divided between wondering whether anyone was still watching us and - more to the point - whether they'd try and stop us from leaving the house and new, fresh thoughts questioning whether it was just father-figures in general that I didn't get on with? Perhaps some kind of alpha-male thing that I have a tendency to fight back against? As memories of my real life come back to me, bit by bit, I realise just how much I had resented my dad. And - living this lie in the house - I hate Father. Maybe I'm the one with the issues?

"What are you thinking?" Sister asked.

She was throwing some clothes into a carrier bag snatched from the kitchen. I don't see the point in packing any belongings. I know that behind that wall - there is a world of new clothes and hot showers waiting. Packing now, especially these clothes, is just a waste of energy. And it's not as though the cat took much of the lingering hunger from me. Definitely better to save the strength.

"Nothing."

"Yes you are. I can see it on your face."

She set the bag down and sat next to me.

"What is it?"

Where to start? I have issues in both this world and the real world out there? Or do I start by telling her we're living a lie? Blurt out that we're not family? Tell her there was no bomb and that - in actual fact - the world is ticking along just as it was before? Or do I tell her that I keep thinking I'm going to have to kill Father before he hurts one of us? I can't tell her anything. My thoughts are my own, even though I wish I were able to share them; if only to lighten the burden. She can't be trusted though. She can't. She'll tell him. And then it will all kick off.

"It's nothing. Really. I'm just tired."

She didn't take her eyes from mine. She could tell I was lying. It was obvious despite my best intentions to hide it from her. Part of me started to wonder whether I could share some of it with her. Part of me wondered whether, since coming home, she'd grown a little more attached to me and that she might be able to keep a secret after all - maybe even help me to figure it all out? She sided with me downstairs. If memory serves correctly, I think that could have been the first time she had done so. I think.

"Come on. I'm your sister…"

No you're not.

"… Let me help you. We're in this together," she continued.

I sighed.

"Can you keep a secret?" I asked.

"Yes."

"You promise?"

"Yes. What is it?"

⅄

A POSSIBLE FUTURE

I had a final look around the bedroom to see if there was anything I had forgotten to pack. The place looks as though a bomb has hit it. Quite ironic really considering the bomb was supposed to hit outside. Out there is clear, blue skies and sunshine. Inside here is chaos and disarray. Part of me will be glad to see the back of this shit-hole.

Satisfied that nothing of value was left, I turned for the door and jumped back when I realised Father was standing there watching me. His arms folded, a look of disdain on his face.

"Didn't realise you were there," I said.

He didn't say anything. I had a sinking feeling in my heart as I realised the secret I had asked Sister to keep had already been revealed to anyone who'd listen.

"No bomb?" he said.

His voice was low. Menacing. Threatening.

I didn't say anything.

"Your sister told me what you said to her. What? Is that some kind of sick joke? Are you trying to be funny? Trying to get her hopes up before we leave the house?"

"No. It's the truth."

"The truth?"

"Yes."

"Out there the world lives on. I made the events about the bomb up? And - I guess - I fabricated the photograph of us as a family too?"

"Not you. Them."

27

"Ah, yes. She did say something about them. Scientists? Government bodies? Something about a test - how would normal folk react in an end of the world type scenario? Yes?"

"Something like that."

"I actually wish it was true."

"It is."

"Because then - at least - you wouldn't be my son."

Father learns the truth of the situation from Sister's loose lips and he's grateful because it means I'm not his son? He's not grateful for the lack of bomb, or the fact that everything - out there - is unharmed and our old lives are out there waiting for us to continue with them?

Without any further words he lunged forward and hit me in the face. I dropped to the floor - a thudding, jarring pain in my jaw where his fist had connected. I didn't have time to react, not before the fist hit me and not afterwards either. He was on top of me before I had even finished sliding along the floor. He landed blow after blow on my face. So much speed, so much anger. I couldn't focus on anything as each hit connected. Everything was getting darker. Even the words he shouted - something about being ashamed and no son of his and something about them being better off without me - even the words echoed into a mishmash of confusion.

I found myself standing by the door. Father and I were on the other side of the room. He was still hitting me. I wasn't even struggling under his weight now. My body was limp. Lifeless. From the door, I started shouting at Father to leave me alone - to get off me - but I knew he didn't hear me. Even if he had - he wasn't going anywhere. Only I was.

The walls around the room burst into flames. Laughter and screaming - not of this Earth - echoed throughout the house. This is it. This is Hell. I screamed as loudly as I could but nothing came from my mouth.

A low growl from behind me caught my attention. I span around and saw Sister standing at the far end of the landing. At least it had Sister's face. A red, naked body. Muscular. Large. A tail. Fork on the end. Pert breasts. What the fuck is this? What the fuck is going on? I went to back away but it lunged towards me at such a pace that it was soon next to me - its hands on my shoulders forcing me to my knees. I screamed again but no sound came from my mouth. Only an erect penis entered it. Severed. Rotten. Pushed there by the Devil Sister. Its low growled voice telling me how much it wanted me to taste its cock. I tried to pull away from it - and for a moment I even managed, twisting my head to the side. Father still in the corner beating my lifeless body more than is deserved. The Devil Sister twisted my head back to face it as it leaned in close to me. The stench of old semen in its breath. It pulled the cock from my mouth and threw it to the corner of the room where it landed - unnoticed by Father. A low growl from the monster ordering me to kiss it as it forced its tongue into my mouth. I tried to resist but couldn't as it held my mouth open with large, powerful hands. The Devil Sister's stomach gurgled loudly and its eyes widened as it started to violently sick up into my mouth. Its tongue snaked its way down my throat, holding it open as the sick poured down into the depths of my stomach. I wanted to scream. Oh, how I wanted to scream.

.⅄.

NOW

Secrets and Lies
"Well?"

Sister's voice pulled me back to reality.

She continued, "What's the secret?"

I couldn't tell her anything. I wanted to trust her so badly but I couldn't. And to try would be foolish. I'm in this alone. Even if they did believe me (before I showed them the wall), there's no guarantee they won't react with hostility for keeping it secret for so long. I could explain - try at least - but there's no way I can be sure they'll care to listen to explanations. Regardless - I needed a 'secret' to tell her.

"I'm scared," I told her after a slight hesitation.

She smiled sympathetically, "Me too."

Father's voice boomed up the stairs, "Come on! We're leaving!"

"What if we stay here?" I asked Sister.

"What?"

"What if we don't go with them. You heard him - it's up to us. We could stay. Just the two of us. Let them go. If they find help, or anyone out there - I'm sure they'll send for us."

"I'm not sure."

"If we leave - if we go out there - I think it will lead to trouble. You've seen how Father is becoming. He is unhinged. He is getting worse. He killed a cat for fuck sake."

"To survive…"

"No. Don't. That cat made no bearing as to whether we survive, or not. There was hardly any meat on it. He could have gone out there and picked berries off trees which would have given us more nutrition. He did it just to mess with our heads… On the road - what else will he do?"

"But no one has been by for a few days now. There's been nothing. We're alone."

"And that's probably for the best. If we starve, we starve but… At least we'll die human. We go with him - them - there's no guarantees we will find anything out there to help us. Chances are we will find nothing but danger and death. I've seen it out there, it's not pretty…"

"But we have to try…"

I couldn't understand why she'd sided with me downstairs only to be sure she wanted to leave now. I could tell by her face she was confused. A mess. We all were.

"One minute you want out of the house and the next you want to stay," she pointed out.

"Because I've seen what is out there. Trust me. You don't want to go. It will change everything for us."

"COME ON!" Father screamed.

"We should go downstairs," Sister said. "He'll get angry."

She turned and went to walk towards the door. I reached out and grabbed her by the arm. She span to face me.

"What are we going to tell him?" I asked. "Are we staying?"

She shook her head.

"I'm sorry but I think we should go."

"Earlier you said…"

"I know what I said but - the cat…"

"… The one he killed."

"If that cat was out there living happily then… Maybe we'll find some people doing the same thing? Maybe we'll find sanctuary somewhere else? Food at the very least?"

"KIDS!" Father's voice echoed up the stairs.

"If there's a chance to survive - I want it," Sister said.

She pulled away from my grip and hurried from the room. I reluctantly followed, unsure of what else I can do to stop them.

CHAPTER 4

BEFORE

Leaving

I **was sitting** on my bed feeling pathetic for crying. I felt like a young, stupid sixteen year old in love. More specifically I felt like a young, stupid sixteen year old who'd just had his still-beating heart ripped from his chest and thrust back into his face. I loved her. I love her. How can she do this to me?

My girlfriend was sitting opposite me. The look on her face suggested she didn't care the pain she was causing me. She didn't even seem to care to hear my argument either; one trying to get her to stay with me. She wanted gone and that was that. Her mind was made up and there was seemingly nothing I could do about it even though there was a small part of my brain screaming at me that - if I were to smash her head in - she could never leave. She'd be with me forever.

I wiped the tears from my cheeks and tried my damnedest to compose myself. Whatever her reason was for leaving - other than the old classic that it wasn't me but her - at least she did it face to face. She could have done it via text message, or even more cowardly, by letter. She stood up and picked her black jacket from the back of the chair tucked up against my desk and threw it on.

I should have seen this coming - she's been off for a while now. I'd tell her that I loved her and she'd reply that she knew. And then there was sex. I'd make a move towards her, she'd make a move away stating she had a headache, or that it was her time. She came to visit me still but - despite this - she was distant. Cold.

And now I knew why.

I stood up too and watched helplessly as she walked to the bedroom door. She opened it.

"Wait!"

She hesitated in the doorway. Didn't turn to look at me though. I wasn't even worth that much.

"There's nothing I can say that will stop you from leaving is there?"

Still without turning, she shook her head. Without any further words she stepped from my bedroom and headed for the stairs and out of my life. I'd even tried to keep her as a friend. We started out as mates and it felt a shame to throw that away too. She declined though. She said I would thank her in the long run. Friendship between exes doesn't work. There's always one who wants more than the other. She'd probably be worried that I'd meet up with her new boyfriend and cook him…

And - half an hour after her coming round - I was single. Jobless, no money, no love life. Have to start questioning what the point is.

I closed my bedroom door and retreated back to my bed.

$$\blacktriangle$$

NOW

Echoes from my Past

The previous memory of my ex-girlfriend hit me like a spade to the face as I made my way down the stairs after Sister. The biggest part of the memory was not the act of getting dumped though - as painful as it was - but rather it was the quick, dirty thought of what I could do to get her to stay with me; bash her brains in. The violent tendencies lurking there in my moment of pain - were they always there, waiting to come out? When that man came around the house - the one I had killed… I had been surprised by that. Maybe I shouldn't have been. Maybe it would have been more apt to be surprised if I hadn't lashed out.

"Where's your stuff?"

Father was standing by the front door, car keys in hand. He was staring right at me. A look of hope - I'm sure - in his face that I was about to tell him that I wasn't going with them and that I was staying behind.

Sister and Mother also turned.

"I don't need anything."

Father's face seemed to drop when he realised I was going with them. Sister's - on the other hand - seemed relieved. Father stormed out to the car, followed by Mother. Sister approached me and put her arms around me.

"I thought you were going to say you weren't coming," she said.

"I still think it's a bad idea but... I didn't want you going out there alone."

I wondered if it sounded as cheesy as it felt. I tried to shake it from my mind.

"Let's go!" Father called from the car. He was standing by the boot, with it open ready for Sister's bag.

We stepped out of the house and slammed the door behind us.

"I actually feel a little bit nervous," Sister said to me.

"Everything will be fine," I lied.

I wanted to ask Sister what would happen to us - what would become of our relationship - if we were to find somewhere else. If we stumbled across another camp within these walls, for example, would she and I still... act... the same as we have been acting here? Or would we revert back to being a 'normal' brother and sister couple? I didn't like the idea of that. The idea of going from being able to do as I choose to not being able to touch her without someone judging us. But then - I guess our relationship is doomed anyway. If we stay here, we will most likely die, in time. And if we leave and find another 'survivalist group' within the compound - we'll most likely go back to a non-sexual relationship and then there's the final outcome; escaping this Hell-hole and trying to fit back into a normal society. She'll never want to see me again. Whichever path we tread - as lovers - she is lost to me. That same feeling I experienced on the bed with my girlfriend, before my world got turned to shit, ripped through me as my heart sank.

Sister put her bag in the boot and jumped into the back of the car.

Mother was standing near to the car. She was being weird - staring up at the blue skies above.

"You okay Mother?" I asked her.

She'd been strange for days to be fair. The strain of our situation clearly too much for her mind to comprehend. Had we stayed, I honestly believe she would have ended up taking her own life or simply going crazy. I mean proper crazy. The type of crazy which sees you run around the house having to hide anything that's sharp...

Hell - for her own safety - maybe put her in a house in the middle of the country and brick her inside. Make sure there are no sharp implements in there at all.

"Beautiful, isn't it?" she said.

"What?"

"This. The world."

I knew the truth - that the world was being run by sick bastards who'd happily conduct experiments on innocent people just because they have too much time on their hands and a dark curiosity to feed. Mum didn't know that. She only knew the truth they'd been fed; the world had ended and everything had gone to shit. Whichever viewpoint you see the world through - neither of them can be described as beautiful.

"I guess," it was easier to go along with her.

"Just think, somewhere out there people can't see this sight. The blue skies, the lack of smog." She sighed, "We should be thankful. At least, here, we have this to see."

"More reason to stay," I told her.

Father shot me a look, "Hurry up and get in the car!"

"We're going," Mother said. "We need to make the most of this sight. Really take it in. After all, we don't know what is waiting for us."

"We do, though. Death is waiting for us," I lied.

In truth normality was waiting for us. As we stood here looking up at the clear skies on this perfect day, you can bet - not more than ten minutes from this location - there are people bunking from college, school or work to enjoy a sneaky trip to the local beaches or parks. People living their lives, enjoying the heatwave, tucking into refreshing ice-creams...

A set of keys hit me in the chest and dropped to the floor. I picked them up. They were the car keys. Father had thrown them at me.

"You can drive," he said.

"What?"

"Show us what you found?"

Father climbed into the passenger seat and even Mother took her own seat in the car - at the back next to where Sister was patiently waiting. I climbed in and slammed the door shut. I slid the key into the ignition and turned to Father.

"I still think this is a bad idea," I said.

"And when we're all dying - having been attacked by whatever is out there… I give you my full permission to say I told you so," he sneered at me.

I sighed and fired the engine up. Thinking back to the saying that every cloud has a silver lining I can't help but breathe a sigh of relief that at least I am driving us around. I'll be able to drive us around the compound for a while, try and stay away from the wall blocking us in.

A quick check of the petrol gauge shows I'll have to do a lot of circles but it's still a possibility that I could drive us around long enough for us to run out of petrol. Then we'll have no choice but to house up in one of the other homes around here. Probably end up starving to death but - it's better than letting them discover the truth. Jesus - the way I reacted out there… I killed that technician. He was helping me. He was helping me remember and see what happened to us - what was happening to us… And… I killed him. Messily. God only knows how they'll react out there.

"What are you waiting for?" Father asked.

"Trying to remember the way," I said.

I was trying to remember the way; trying to recall the way to the wall. Need to know which direction to head away from.

"You know the old saying," Father said.

"What do you mean?"

He turned to me, "All roads lead to Rome."

He nodded towards the end of the driveway. Reluctantly, I pushed my foot down on the accelerator.

"Well - this is exciting, isn't it?" Mother chirped from the back of the car. She wasn't excited. None of us were. We were all apprehensive; them because they didn't know what was waiting for them out here and me - because I knew exactly what was out there. Ah ha. Just remembered. The house. The one I found before finding the exit to the compound; with the dead couple in their bed. The two who'd chosen suicide as their way out. I'll take the family (not my family) there. They'll go in, see the dead bodies and realise there's nothing out here. With any luck, they'll have another vote. I can always instigate one. See if I can get them to say they'll come back to our own house…

I sped up. Higher the rev counter, faster I drive… Higher the fuel consumption.

"I'm sorry if you think I've just been going against everything you've suggested," I said to Father. It dawned on me that all I had been doing recently was banging heads with Father. I wasn't in the wrong to do so. Someone had to. But... if I carried on banging heads with him, continued to go against everything he said, then we would never agree on a plan of action. At least, we'll never agree on one that I put forward. It dawned on me that I need to give a little before I can expect to take.

Father didn't say anything. I glanced to the side to see if he was even listening. He was staring out of the passenger window. Here I am - trying to make peace - and he wasn't even paying me any attention.

"Did you hear me?" I asked him.

"I did."

"Oh. Okay."

Heard me. Chose to ignore me. So much for our bonding time. I looked into the rear-view mirror to see if anyone else was paying attention to this. They too were looking out of their windows, trapped in their own thoughts or just not wanting to get involved. Not sure which.

"Did you try the radio?" he asked.

"Broken," I said.

"Shame."

He leaned down and fiddled with the dial. True to my word - it didn't work. This is the point where I had to fight with myself not to say I told you so. I flashed him a look - hoping the expression on my face spoke the words I dare not.

It's going to be a long car journey.

⋏

BEFORE

Not in Control

Dad was driving me somewhere. He hadn't said where. He'd just told me that we had somewhere to be. I didn't argue with him. I couldn't be bothered. Still pining over my girlfriend (or rather, lack of). I was looking out of the window, wondering where we were going. Dad leaned down to the radio quietly pumping tunes into the car, and killed it with a flick of the switch.

"Where are we going?" I asked him.

"For a drive."

"A drive? I thought you said we had somewhere to be?"

"We do."

I laughed at how awkward he was being, "So where are we going?"

We turned into a small car-park illuminated only by a couple of lights at either side of it. He pulled up underneath one of them and switched the car's interior light on. I looked out of the window. I knew the car-park but had never been in it before and - more to the point - I couldn't see anything nearby which would warrant us being here.

My over-active imagination started whispering evil thoughts to me; he's brought you somewhere quiet and is finally going to kill you.

The only thing he killed was the engine.

"What are we doing?"

"We're talking."

"Talking?"

Dad nodded.

"Couldn't we have done this at home where it is warm?"

Dad shook his head.

"No?"

"No."

"Okay. What did you want to talk about?"

"How long have you been out of employment for now?" he asked.

His question came out of the blue and took me by surprise. Of all the things for him to ask - at this particular moment - this wasn't one of the possibilities that I expected to come from his mouth.

"Few months?"

"Four."

"Four?"

"Four months."

"Seems like quite a while."

"Know how much you have contributed to the household in those four months?"

"When I've had a little extra money left over from my benefits, I've given mum…"

Dad interrupted me, "Twenty-five pounds…"

"Twenty-five?"

"You think that's fair?"

"Well the benefits money doesn't tend to go very far."

"Yet you still manage to go out with your friends…"

"Rarely."

"Yet you still go out."

I didn't argue with him. There was simply no point. I shifted uncomfortably in my seat wondering where this was going and - more to the point - why we couldn't have done this at home.

"You're going to have to move out," dad broke the silence.

"What? You want me to move out?"

"It's for the best."

"Not for me it isn't."

It suddenly dawned on me why he had pulled me away from the house to have this conversation. This was all his idea. He pulled me out of the comfort of our home so mum couldn't hear what he had to say. I'd wager a bet she didn't even know he planned to say this.

"Does mum know we're having this conversation?" I asked him.

He glared at me, "And she won't know."

"She'll have a good guess. I'm just expected to go home, pack up my bits and move out with nowhere to go? You really think she won't suspect something is up?"

"If you want one thousand pounds and to stay in my will - I'm pretty sure you can make it so she doesn't expect anything."

"A thousand pounds?"

Dad nodded, "Something to help you set yourself up in a new flat."

"How do you expect me to keep a flat if I don't have a job? What, I pay one month of rent and then that's it - I'm evicted with nowhere to go?"

"Gives you some extra drive. A little focus."

"What have I done to make you hate me so much?"

Dad didn't answer me. In truth - I guess I didn't expect him to.

"So how long have I got?" I asked him.

"I'll give you until the end of the week," he said.

"The end of the week?"

It was Friday evening.

Dad nodded.

"How am I supposed to find a new place to live in a couple of days?" I asked.

Dad smiled, "Not my problem."

⅄

NOW

"What's that?" I nodded out of the windscreen towards a building in the distance. Of course I knew exactly what it was; the house where I had found the old couple in their bed - having taken their own lives rather than try and survive in this shitty situation.

Chapter 5

NOW

Home From Home

"Just keep driving," Father said.

Funnily enough I hadn't counted on him telling me to just keep driving. I thought a curious streak in him would make him want to stop off and investigate the property. I slowed the car down to a crawl despite what he said.

"What are you doing?" he asked. "Didn't you hear me?"

I had to think on my feet. Had to convince him it would be a good idea to stop and look around.

"We need to stop," I said.

"We've only just started, keep going."

"I've seen it out there. The place is a wreck. We need to see if there is any food here," I said despite knowing full well that the cupboards were bare.

"I am hungry," Mother piped up from the back.

Father knew what I was saying made sense but there was a strong chance he'd go against it regardless - for no other reason than to be an asshole to me. With Mother getting involved from the back, even as indirectly as saying she was hungry, there was more of a possibility Father would permit us to pull over to search the property.

"Make it quick," Father said in a hushed voice as though he didn't want anyone in the back to hear he had agreed with me. I wanted to bask in the moment.

I wanted to ask him to repeat himself a little louder; pretend I hadn't heard him. I didn't though. Figured it best to say nothing.

I pulled the car to a complete stop just by the front door. I killed the engine and slid the key from the ignition. Not sure why I took the key back. It wasn't as though anyone was going to take the car from us.

I looked at Father and asked, "How do you want to do this?"

"Quickly and quietly."

We hadn't seen anyone for a couple of days now - other than the cat - and still Father was concerned about running into trouble. I didn't question his thought processes. No sense picking an argument. I faced the girls sitting in the back.

"Ready?" I asked them.

"Ready for what? They're not coming with us!" Father said.

"What are you talking about?"

"They need to stay here, with the car. Make sure no one takes it."

"Who? Who exactly? We haven't seen anyone. Not back at our home, not on the way here... We're alone. You know it makes sense for them to come in. It'll take less time to look around if we're all in there."

"They're staying in the car. End of discussion."

Father opened the door and climbed from the car. He slammed the door shut. I hesitated a moment wondering what I could say to get him to change his mind about taking the girls in. He was already at the front door. Can't think of anything. Damn. I turned back to the girls, "We won't be long."

I opened the door and climbed from the car, following Father. Before I had even reached him, he was knocking on the door.

"You think anyone is home?" I asked. "The place looks empty."

"Doesn't hurt to be safe. If there is anyone in there - and we go bursting in... They probably won't respond too kindly."

We waited for a while to see if anyone would come and answer the door. Frustrating considering I knew there was no one home. At least - no one who was still breathing. Father reached down with his left hand and tried the door. I wasn't surprised when it opened. He pushed the door open and stepped in. He turned his head back towards where I was standing. I could tell by the look on his face that the smell of the elderly couple had hit him and that he was trying to get the last bit of possible fresh air before being completely overcome. I took a deep breath myself and stepped into the dark hall, leaving the door open behind me in the hope it would encourage a fresh breeze to run through the rooms.

"Fucking stinks," Father said as he made his way through to the kitchen.

I followed wishing he had gone to investigate upstairs first. The sooner he sees the bodies up there, tucked up in bed together in a final embrace, the sooner I can try and convince him it's a good idea to get out of here and go home again.

"Check the cupboards over there!" he ordered me as he started working from one side of the kitchen, pulling all the various cupboards and drawers open in the search for food. In order to keep up appearances, I did the same from the opposite end of the kitchen just as he had instructed. I knew there was nothing in here though. I knew this was a waste of time. Couldn't say anything though. "Well - son - this was a brilliant idea you had," Father mocked me.

"It was worth a look," I replied.

Father stopped what he was doing and smirked, "No. It wasn't."

I changed the subject back to the purpose of why I had brought him here in the first place, "What's that fucking smell?"

Father shrugged, "Not our concern. We need to get going whilst it's still light outside."

He pushed passed me and headed back down the hallway towards the front door (and the ever enticing fresh air).

"You're leaving?" I called out.

"We stopped for food. There is none. There's clearly no survivors. We need to go."

Father didn't wait for me to argue with him. He was already out the front door. I muttered under my breath and followed him - happy to be out in the fresh air but disappointed he hadn't seen the elderly couple rotting in their bed. My heart sank further when I noticed he'd climbed into the driver's seat. I didn't say anything. I just climbed into the passenger side with a feeling of dread washing over me. With Father behind the wheel, it's only a matter of time before he discovers the truth and they all realise I had been lying to them. No. Not lying. I just hadn't told them the whole truth… Either way - relationships are going to change.

⋏

BEFORE

Own Two Feet

I was standing in the empty living room of what had recently become my new flat. One month's rent paid by dad and some money in my bank account for the following months too. To be paid back of course - in full. There were no freebies.

Mum was looking at me, tears in her eyes. Dad was standing by the front door.

"What do you think?" I asked her.

I was asking about the flat. This was the first time mum had seen it. Only the second time I had seen it. Third time for dad who'd agreed to it before even showing me. I don't think he believes it's necessarily the best deal but it was available immediately and - to him - that's all that mattered.

"Mum?"

"It's…. Nice."

She didn't like it. I don't blame her. I didn't either. It was small. Cramped. Ugly. Smelt funny. Crap view out of the windows too; some dodgy looking industrial estate where girls plied their trade late at night.

Mum turned to me, "Are you sure you want this?" she asked.

"I like it."

I hate it. Dad liked it. I didn't get a choice in the matter.

"It'll be fine when he moves his stuff in. Very homely," dad called from the doorway.

"He's right," I tried to reassure mum. "It'll be good."

"I like having you at home," she said.

I smiled at her and gave her a hug. As I held her close, I twisted my head to look at dad. He looked completely indifferent to me. I wondered what I had done to push him away from me. Had he always felt like this? Had he been just waiting for the right moment to kick me out?

"You can still come and visit," mum said.

"Yes. Of course."

I wanted to tell her about dad. I wanted to tell her that I was moving out because he wanted me to and that - in actual fact - I wanted to stay at home with them.

At least until I was more secure on my own two feet. I couldn't say anything though. She loved him and I think he loved her. Who was I to ruin that for her?

Doesn't mean I can't hate him though.

⋏

NOW

The Truth

"You need to pull the car over," I told Father.

He ignored me. He just kept on driving. I reached down and pulled the handbrake up and the car screeched to a halt. Father turned to me - such anger in those black eyes.

"What the fuck is wrong with you?" he asked.

"I need to tell you something before we go any further. It's important."

"Take your hand off the fucking handbrake!" Father shouted.

"No. Not until you listen to what I have to say..."

"What is it?" Mother asked from the back.

Father turned the engine off - no doubt to conserve fuel - and stared at me. We're not family - not real family - and yet the look he has in his eyes, right now, is almost exactly the same look my own dad gave me.

"Well? What is it?" he asked. "What's so important?"

I took a deep breath. I didn't want to tell them. I wanted to keep the truth from them. I knew I couldn't though. They were on the path to finding out for themselves and - if I didn't say anything - they'd never forgive me. Hell - there's a chance they'll never forgive me for keeping it from them anyway.

"There wasn't an explosion," I said.

No easy way of saying it. Just need to spit it out.

"What are you talking about?"

"We're not a real family."

"Of course we are! Don't be so silly!" Mother put her hand on my shoulder as though it were supposed to give me some form of comfort and let her know that she was there for me. Father said nothing. He was just staring at me with those dead eyes.

"It's nothing more than an experiment," I said.

No one said anything. We all just sat there in silence.

Unsurprisingly Father was the first to speak, "Finished?"

He leaned forward and turned the car key in the ignition. The engine growled into life.

"I'm telling you the truth," I said.

"I don't know what you're trying to achieve but... You need to stop it. Seriously - what the fuck is wrong with you?"

"I'm telling you the truth!" I shouted. "I found the site from where they control us. I found the files which told me everything. The memory wipe they performed on us - controlled by a drug in the water... That's why the water was so plentiful. Because they wanted it to be! I found out every..."

"Just shut the fuck up!" Father shouted.

"If you keep driving this road - you're going to reach the very same compound I stumbled across. Everything is there..."

"And if this is true - why did you come back to us?"

Sister suddenly screamed from the back of the car. She opened the car door and started to run back down the dirt track towards the house of death we'd not long since left.

"Now look what you've done."

Father and Mother climbed from the car too before I had a chance to explain why I was telling them this and - to answer his question - why I ended up going back to the house where they'd been hiding away. I hesitated a moment before I too opened the car door and gave chase to Sister. She had run straight into the house in floods of tears. Father was first through the door, followed closely by Mother. By the time I entered, they were all standing in the kitchen. Sister was screaming from the kitchen about not wanting to go on anymore.

"Get back to the car. We need to get going!"

"I don't want to go! I just want to stay here..."

"Come on, honey..." Mother stepped in as though a kinder word would entice Sister back to the car.

"See what you've done?" Father turned to me. Venom in his voice, anger in his eyes.

Mother kept trying to talk Sister down, "Why don't you want to go? You heard your brother - everything is fine out there. He's seen it. There was no bomb. We can go home…"

"I don't remember anything. Before waking up with all of you. I don't recall who I am… How can I go back?" Sister was crying. Her thoughts echoed my own thoughts when I first had found out that the world we were living in was nothing more than a lie. How can you go back when you've been turned into something you don't like? There is no way back.

"He was lying. A sick joke. There was a bomb. The world is broken out there…" Father turned to me, "Tell them. Tell them you were joking. Not that it was very funny."

"No. I wasn't. It was the truth."

Father lunged forward and put his hands around my throat. Before I had a chance to do anything he pushed me back against the wall. I put my hands up to his and tried to pull his grip from my neck but I couldn't. Too weak. I'm not sure if it is the lack of food or the fact he's stronger.

"I don't know what is going on in that fucking head of yours but you need to stop!"

Sister screamed, "Get off him!"

Father turned to her as my vision started to blur, "Shut up, whore!"

He released one hand long enough to smack her across the face. She dropped to the floor with a thud. I tried to get away from him but - even with only one hand around my throat - I still couldn't move. Mother rushed to Sister as Father turned his attention back to me. She screamed for him to stop what he was doing but he wasn't listening. He didn't care about the pain (and fear) he was causing us.

Sister screamed. She got up to her feet and ran for the back door. She pulled it open, ready to make her escape - away from the danger - and screamed again when one of the infected staggered into the room. It was only when Mother also screamed that Father turned to see what the problem was. He released his grip and I slid down the wall onto my arse, gasping for breath. By the time Father crossed the room - the yellow, skinned bastard had a hold of Sister's head and was biting her neck with his black-stained teeth. The black tar spilling from its mouth into the fresh, open wound. Father grabbed the thing by the scruff of its neck and ripped it away from Sister - who fell to the floor as soon as she was free. I pulled myself to my feet and watched in horror as the thing turned and hit Father with a firm back-hander which sent him flying across the room where he slammed into the far wall. Mother screamed as it lurched towards her.

I dashed forward and jumped on the back of the infected. My distraction was enough for Mother to get to the other side of the room. Even Sister had dragged herself away from imminent danger. I - on the other hand - had placed myself right into the thick of it. I'd forgotten how strong these things were. Their yellow skin, their red eyes, the black ooze leaking from their mouths - they look as though as they should be weak and easy to take down. Need to remember these bastards are a government experiment. God only knows the shit flowing through their veins and what it was intended for. A government thing designed to enhance their soldiers that hadn't worked out quite as they had planned?

Father roared as loud as the thing trying to shake me from its back. He ran across the room with a knife, taken from the drawer, and plunged it directly into the thing's throat. A jet of black sprayed from the wound as he withdrew the blade. Father didn't stop there. He stabbed it again - right in the eye. He pulled the blade out and the eye slopped out too. He stabbed it in the forehead and the blade came out with pieces of brain attached. Another stab went through the cheek and another back through the forehead. This time the thing dropped to its knees - me still holding onto its back. Father pulled the knife from the head again and it dropped to the floor - lifeless. I let go of it and stood up. Soon froze again when I realised Father was staring at me - knife in hand - with that look of anger on his face.

"I think it's dead," I said in an effort to snap him back to the present.

"Government experiment?" he asked. "Radiation poisoning from the blast, that's what caused this."

Mother screamed from the other side of the room. I looked to her - as did Father. She was crouched by Sister.

"I think something is wrong!" she shouted at us.

Sister was twitching violently. There was black shit coming from her mouth, just as there had been from the mouth of her attacker.

"What's happening?" Mother screamed.

Father put the knife on the side and hurried over to Sister. He knelt on the floor and pulled Sister up so that she was leaning back on his lap.

Mother screamed again, "What is happening?!"

"I don't know!" Father shouted back. "I don't fucking know!"

I was just standing there. I felt useless. Nothing I could do.

Sister gasped and went limp. Her eyes slowly rolled to the back of her head.

"What's happening? What's she doing? What's going on?" Mother was frantic.

Father didn't move. He just stared down at the body of Sister.

I dreaded the question I had to ask, "Is she... Is she dead?"

Father pushed her body to the side. She slumped onto the floor.

I asked again. I needed to hear it.

"Is she dead?"

Mother started to weep as Father said yes. I felt sick. Was this my fault? Had I not said anything - in the car... Had I not told the truth about our situation... Would she still have been alive? Of course she would. We would all be in the car, right now, heading for the wall. She would have seen it herself. The shock would have been greater but... She would have been alive. It is my fault.

"Maybe you're right," Father said, pulling me back to our current situation. He pulled himself to his feet and stepped away from Sister's corpse as Mother swapped positions with him - clutching the cold body of Sister as tightly as she could. Father was looking at me. Whatever the point he was making, it was between the two of us.

"What?"

"Maybe we're not family." He looked at Sister's body. "I mean, if we were family, surely I'd feel something for this but... I feel nothing. No sense of loss, no grief, no anger at the thing which did this to her. I feel absolutely fuck all."

CHAPTER 6

BEFORE

Home Truths

I was sitting with dad. It was just the two of us. We were in the dining room, waiting for mum to dish up the Sunday Roast. Dad had been off with me from the moment I had walked into 'his' home. I'm guessing my arrival was the first he had known of mum's invitation to dinner. Have to say - conversation wasn't exactly free-flowing.

"Going to be like this every Sunday?" he asked.

"What do you mean?"

"You. Here."

"I'm sorry?"

"Are you planning on coming around here every Sunday? You know - we need to know these things to ensure we have enough food in the house..."

"What? Mum invited me."

"Course she did. What - did you give her the guilt trip? Phone her up complaining about the lack of food in the house? Something like that?"

"No. She phoned me. She asked if I wanted to join you for dinner."

"Haven't even been out of the house for a whole week and yet - here you are - back here. Scrounging."

"I'm not scrounging. I accepted an invitation."

There was silence between the two of us. I took a deep breath and asked the question I had posed before but never really had an answer to, "Was there ever a time when you wanted me around?" I asked.

Dad didn't answer me with words exactly but - the look... The look said it all. I wasn't surprised. What I was surprised about was that I wasn't bothered. He didn't love me. He didn't want me around. It should have hurt to learn this but I didn't care. Maybe it was the constant put downs? Maybe it was always living in his shadow? Maybe I had just gotten used to the idea of not being wanted by him? Not sure. I just didn't care.

Mum walked into the room, a beaming smile on her face, "Dinner is five minutes from being done," she said.

"That's great. Can I give you a hand with anything?" I asked. I hoped she'd say there was something I could do. Anything to get away from staying in dad's poisonous company.

"No, that's fine. You just put your feet up and relax," she said.

She walked from the room, leaving me with dad.

He smiled. He knew why I was offering to help. "So," he said, "got a job yet?"

NOW

Coming to a Head

"What did you say?"

I was staring at Father in utter disbelief. Did he really just say that? He feels nothing that Sister is dead? Even if we aren't family - was there no empathy there for the passing of a fellow human being?

He smirked, "You should be pleased, means I might just start listening to your stories..."

He walked over to the back door - previously opened by Sister - and slammed it shut to stop anymore of the infected wandering in.

"Tell me from the top - and try not to miss anything out - what did you find out there?"

"Now isn't the time..."

"Now is the perfect time. We need to know what we're about to run into…"

"Look!" Mother called out from where she sat with Sister. "She moved. She's not dead! Get a towel, or something, to push against her wound to help stop the bleeding!"

Both Father and I turned to look at what had caught her eye. Sister was indeed twitching. Her head was lolling from side to side. A strange gasping noise coming from her mouth, accompanied by dribbles of black.

"Get away from her!" I dashed forward and pulled Mother away from Sister's convulsing body. She wasn't alive. She was far from it. Whatever was happening to her now - it wasn't good and, more to the point, it wasn't really her. The black stuff oozing from her - it must have had something to do with that. Maybe a contaminate?

We all jumped when Sister bolted upright into a sitting position. Lips curling upwards as she snarled at us. She just sat there looking vacantly around the room. Definitely not Sister anymore.

"Don't just stand there!" Mother said. "Help her up."

Mother made a move to help Sister but I stopped her in her tracks.

"It's not her," I told her.

"Don't be silly. Of course it is," Mother tried to pull away from my grip.

Sister scrambled to her feet.

"It's not her," I repeated.

Father didn't need telling twice. He grabbed the knife from the side and lunged for her sticking it through her eyeball and into her brain. Sister's mouth opened wide and black ooze poured out in a spew of vomit. Mother screamed out loud and lunged for Father, stopped (again) by my vice-like grip on her arm.

"What have you done? What have you done?!" she kept screaming again and again.

I pulled her from the room and slammed the kitchen door on Father. He didn't seem to be fazed by Mother's shouting or the fact he'd just put a knife through his make-believe daughter's eye.

I pushed Mother through to the living room and closed that door too. And then I pulled her in close and hugged her tight. She pulled away from my embrace and moved the settee so it was blocking the doorway. She was screaming that Father had killed Sister. As much as I wanted her to hate Father as much as I did - I couldn't let her think that. He wasn't a good person by any stretch of the imagination but he didn't kill Sister. She was already dead. Killed by the Infected person and then - I don't know - taken over by whatever shit flows through their veins. I tried to reassure her that she had already been killed - not that there was much reassurance to be taken from that.

Father started banging on the closed door when he realised he couldn't get in.

"Let me in!" he said.

Mother shouted, "Go away! Leave us alone!"

"I said open this fucking door!"

"Fuck off!"

It didn't matter what I said to her - she was in a state. Clearly she wanted nothing to do with him now. The sight of him killing Sister being too much for her to handle, especially so soon after he had been throttling me and pushing everyone around. I was the bad guy for lying to them but he had painted himself far worse than I could have ever been perceived. No sense trying to change her mind about him. Get him out of the house. Get him gone from our lives. Let him go his own way and let us go our own way.

"You heard her. Just go. We don't want you here."

There was silence for a moment. He was still there though; the other side of the door.

"If I go," he said after a pause, "I won't be coming back."

Mother was crying but didn't seem to be bothered by what he was saying. I didn't argue with him either. His footsteps clumped down the hallway towards the front door. I moved across the room, to the window, and watched as he left the house and headed back towards the car. Well, when we are ready to go, it looks like we're walking.

I turned to Mother.

"He's gone," I said.

She dropped to her knees in floods of tears.

⋏

BEFORE

Options

"Why don't you leave him?"

I handed mum a cup of tea after she made herself comfortable on the settee in my tiny flat. She thanked me and took a careful sip.

"Well?" I pushed her.

"Because I love him."

"He's an asshole. The way he treats you, the other he treats others... Pisses me off. People just let him get away with it. They don't stand up to him. What are they afraid of?"

Mum set the cup of tea to one side and cast her eyes around the flat. She gave me a look.

"What?" I asked.

"People don't stand up to him? You mean - the way you did when you 'decided' to move out and go it alone?"

"This was my choice," I corrected her.

She nodded. We both knew it hadn't been my choice to live in this shit-hole.

"I just think things would be better for everyone if he just vanished," I changed the subject.

⋏

NOW

Old Habits

Mother and I were still in the living room of the abandoned house. I was sitting on the sofa. She was laying next to me with her head in my lap. I was stroking her hair; gently running my hand through it with a soft tenderness. She had calmed down now. Had taken a while. Her head must have been spinning; the news that this whole situation was brought about by a forced government test, the fact we weren't family and now one of us was dead and one of us had (thankfully) vanished into the outside world beyond the four walls of this house and possibly the four walls of the compound too.

"Do you think he will come back?" she asked; her voice breaking the comfortable silence.

"Did you want him to?" I asked.

She didn't say anything. I didn't know the answer to the question I posed. Not how she felt about it anyway. All I knew was that I didn't want him coming back. I wanted him long gone. Didn't even care if he found himself running around in the outside world. As long as he wasn't near me - I didn't give a shit.

"Just the two of us now," she said.

I nodded, not that she saw. We fell into another comfortable silence.

"Did you love her?" she asked.

I knew she was talking about Sister.

"I had feelings for her," I said.

"Even though she wasn't your sister?"

"Yes."

Mother fell silent again. I didn't have anything to say either as my mind drifted to thoughts of Sister. I wondered whether she'd have stuck with me - out there in the real world - or whether she'd have moved on with her life and tried to forget about me (us) and the things that we had done. Guess I'll never know.

"Who was she?" Mother asked.

I tried hard to remember her real name; the one I read in that file. I couldn't recall it. Nor could I recall Mother's real name, or even Father's. I remembered mine but that was mostly because my own memories were slowly coming back to me - even though they weren't necessarily wanted.

"I can't remember," I admitted after a few more seconds of frantically trying to recall her name. I was already dreading the next question.

"And who am I?"

"I don't remember. I'm sorry."

She turned so that her head was facing me.

"Maybe it's a blessing?" she said.

"What?"

"You not remembering who we are. Maybe that's a good thing. Gives us a chance to start again. Be whoever we want to be. You said this was a government experiment?"

"That's right."

"Well - we must have signed up for it."

"We did."

"Then our lives couldn't have been that good to start with."

I knew mine wasn't; debt, father issues, lack of girlfriend... Couldn't say the same for Mother though but - going by my own life - she was probably right.

"So - just the two of us then - we can be whoever we want to be," she continued.

"Yes. We can."

"And you can stop calling me Mother."

Her hand moved up to my crotch. She started rubbing it through my jeans.

"What are you doing?" I asked.

With everything going on in our lives, currently, this was the last thing I thought she would have wanted. She shushed me quiet as she started to fumble with the buttons keeping my jeans closed and my cock out of her hands.

"Go with it," she sighed.

She managed to undo my jeans. She reached into my pants and pulled out my penis. It hadn't taken much for it to become erect. Never did when I had someone touching it. She gave it a flick of her tongue and I closed my eyes. There was nothing stopping us from doing this. We weren't son and mother. There was no reason why we couldn't be lovers. No reason at all - especially seeing as it was just the two of us and especially after everything we have gone through together. My cock slid to the back of her throat and I gasped in delight. No reason at all as to why we shouldn't be doing this. She took my hand as my brain continued its feeble attempts at convincing me that this was the acceptable thing to do. She reached down with it and made me touch her between her legs. I didn't need further prompting. I pulled away from the gentle grip of her hand and slid my hand between leggings, knickers and skin until I was touching her (wet) pussy. She let my cock slide from her mouth as she took her turn to sigh and enjoy the feeling of my fingers sliding into her cunt. I suddenly stopped.

"Wait a minute."

I tried to sit up but had nowhere to go - not with her head in my lap.

"What?"

"There are cameras everywhere. Small ones so that they can watch us…"

"So? Let them watch!"

She took my cock in her mouth again. Another sigh escaped my lips. Feels so fucking good and - slowly - all other thoughts disappeared from my mind. I slid my hand back to her pussy and inserted two fingers at first and - then - a third… Again, my cock slipped from her mouth as she looked up to my face. I opened my fingers up, stretching her lips as wide as my fingers would permit. She writhed around, pushing herself down onto my digits as she went back to expertly working my shaft with her mouth and tongue. I withdrew my fingers long enough to give them a lick. Current predicament had clearly not affected her libido as they were already coated in a layer of her salty cream. I licked my fingers clean before putting them back inside her - thrusting in and out as though actually fucking her with my hard-on.

"How many is that?" she asked.

"Three."

"More."

She put me back in her mouth.

I reached further down to make it easier to move about. I pulled out of her sopping vagina slightly in order to reposition my finger and - soon - I had managed to slip a fourth inside her. She moaned as I opened my fingers up and closed them again - repeating the gesture over a dozen times or so (I wasn't actually counting). A little more repositioning and I struggled to get the thumb inside her too. Not sure whether it's the angle or whether she is too tight but fisting definitely wasn't on the cards today. She took hold of my shaft and started to wank it hard and fast as I continued penetrating her with my fingers.

The look on her face - a completely different woman to the one who'd been weeping less than an hour beforehand. She was more like the woman I'd grown used to living with, back in the other house. The lustful, dirty whore with a strong appetite for flesh and fucks.

She pulled herself away from my hand and my fingers slid from her pussy. She stood, for a moment, to kick off her leggings and stained knickers, before climbing back onto the sofa (and me), lowering her cunt onto my penis. It slid in with ease as I felt her lips embrace my shaft. A second later, no doubt so she could get used to the sensation, she started to ride me with vigour. Neither of us were saying anything now. Both just going with the motion and sensations running through our bodies. I kept my eyes fixed upon her for every time I closed them I imagined it was sister's cunt swallowing my cock and a wave of disappointment would wash over me when I remembered it wasn't.

"I'm going to cum," she breathed heavily.

Her face was flushed as her body started to tremble, whilst she continued to rock it backwards and forwards, up and down. As soon as her orgasm had finished flowing through her body, she slowed to a steady pace. I took a hold of her shoulders and pushed her to the side. My penis slid from her as she fell back to the side of the sofa.

"What are you doing?" she asked. "Did you cum too?"

I didn't reply. I merely repositioned myself so that I was standing next to where her face was on the sofa; my erection a few inches from her face. I started wanking it furiously. My eyes closed. My thoughts on Sister, the one I loved. My orgasm built fairly quickly as I felt Mother's hands cup my balls. A tingling in the thighs... Here it cums... I moaned out loud as stream after sticky stream of semen spat from my bell-end over Mother's waiting (and surprised) face. A sticky end to an already messy situation. I collapsed on the sofa next to her.

"Holy shit!" she laughed as she wiped her face with the back of her hand. "Clearly you needed that as much as I did..."

I didn't say anything. Once again I found myself in a state of confusion. Sister was dead. Her body most likely still warm, maybe even still twitching. Father has left - gone God only knows where, and worse yet, most likely to be extremely dangerous to those he meets and Mother... Mother has gone from grieving, to hating, to fucking within the space of a couple of hours. Looking at her semen-coated face now there's no sign of grief in those eyes of hers. There's nothing but insatiable lust and an obvious hunger.

"What's wrong?" she asked. No doubt she has seen I'm not smiling, like I usually did after an orgasm. I tried to hide my discontented look but clearly failed. "You didn't enjoy that?" she continued.

"It was nice," I said. Must keep the peace.

"Nice?"

"Good."

"Good?"

"Great. Jesus. I'm just   "

"What is it?"

"I don't understand how we got here," I said. "Everything seems to have happened fast; one minute we're heading off to find whatever, the next Father is attacking me, then Sister is being attacked and killed, then Sister is sitting up again and Father is attacking her, you're weeping and screaming for him to leave and then - boom - we're fucking. I'm sorry - I had a great time - but it's a lot to process in such a short time."

"You think too much," Mother said. Words which had been said of my character before now - and not just from Mother. Sister had also told me I think too much. She said that I worried about the little things and turned them into much bigger problems than they really were. I didn't agree with her at the time but maybe she was right. Sister was dead. That eliminates the question of what happens to 'us' when we get out of here and back to the real world and Father has left us which - in turn - eliminates the problem of having to deal with him and the constant clashing. Mother's change in character? Well I guess I'd sooner have someone wanting sex with me compared to someone needing reassurance that everything is going to be okay - especially when I can make no such promises - and continually crying. Perhaps what happened - for whatever reason - is for the best.

I got up from the sofa and rearranged my clothes, putting my cock back into my pants and doing my jeans up. Mother also rearranged her state of undress until she was as decent as can be for a woman coated in slowly drying spunk.

"So what do we do now then?" I asked.

"You said it was a government experiment. Well - I think now we go and get us some compensation," she said.

"And Father?"

"What about him?"

"What do we do about him?" I asked.

He had left - yes - but I didn't like the idea of him out there by himself. Not because I was worried about him - no - but because I was worried about what he was going to do to those he stumbled across. He - like the rest of us - is damaged beyond repair. Out there in the real world, if he continues behaving the way he has been, he is likely to kill more people than I care to think about. And whilst I don't necessarily care about the assholes at the compound - I don't want him walking the streets - the real ones - killing people who have no idea what we have been going through.

"He left us," Mother said. A coldness in her tone. "We owe him nothing."

CHAPTER 7

BEFORE

A Cry for Help

I was standing in front of a chair in my living room. The noose was tied around my neck. I'm no good at tying knots so I just kept tying them until I was one hundred percent confident the rope wouldn't come away from my neck once I stepped from the chair. I wanted it to stay tight. I wanted it to choke the air from my lungs and suffocate me. I had read - on the Internet - that there was a kind of knot you could tie, for this very purpose, that when you hang someone, it actually breaks their neck. The Internet did show images of the knot and I did try to follow them, so I too could have a quicker death than choking it out, but I couldn't figure it out. The whole damned thing was so complicated. In the end I gave up and settled for choking. At the end of the day they both have the same desired effect, right?

On the floor, next to the chair, was a plain white envelope with the word 'mum' written on it. The letter was an apology to her. It wasn't an apology for me taking my own life. It was a 'sorry you're stuck with him' type of apology. It also gave details as to the type of funeral I wanted. I wanted a quiet affair with her and a few of my friends (not that I really see them since splitting with my girlfriend). That was the problem with couples having the same friends; when a break-up does happen, they always pick sides. Not sure why they chose to side with her. She was the one who dumped me. I would have thought they would have called her the bitch and been there for me in my hour of need but - no - apparently not. Oh well. Not long left on this planet to give a shit about trivial things like that. Fuck them.

And fuck him.

He - dad - wasn't permitted at my funeral. He didn't want me in his house, and I respected that, so - in turn - I don't want him at my funeral. I don't want him having the chance to say goodbye to me. I especially don't want him having the opportunity to gloat over my cold corpse. He isn't allowed anywhere near the service.

I climbed onto the chair. The other end of the rope was tied to one of the rafters above me - just through the latch, in the loft. The plan was simple; step off the chair and dance the merry jig on the end of the hangman's rope. Not sure how long it will take exactly. Not sure how much pain will be involved. I'm hoping it's minimal pain and that I lose consciousness fairly promptly. I should have Googled that too when I Googled the best type of knot to use.

Pretty high up here, standing on this chair.

Looking down to where I'm about to start swinging I can already tell it's going to hurt. Come on. It won't hurt for long. Just step off. Let the noose do its job. You can do this. One small step and that is it. Game over. Come on, come on, come on... I took a deep breath.

I closed my eyes.

I lifted my foot from the chair and positioned it as though about to take a step.

This is it.

No more dad.

No more crappy love-life.

No more money problems.

No more feeling of isolation.

Just blackness.

And pain.

And a slow death, swinging around on the end of the rope.

Fuck.

I put my foot down on the chair again. Can't do it. Fucking stupid. I should have just dropped a toaster in the bathtub with me. It would have been easier. Certainly quicker. Damn it. What am I doing? Just get down. Get down from here before you hurt yourself. And mum - imagine if she were the one to find you here... A parent shouldn't need to see that. Ever.

I reached up to the knot and started working it - in an effort to undo it. Crap this thing is tight...

λ

NOW

Can't Go On

Mother and I were still in the living room of the empty house. We had decided to stay here for the night. I say 'we' but it had been my choice. I knew - on foot - we wouldn't get to where we needed to be before the sun went down. We discussed it briefly but neither of us wanted to be out there at night. Not with the Infected out there.

I was standing by the window looking out into the world beyond. Mother was sitting on the sofa - having come back from the bathroom where she'd cleaned her face from what could have been my children had they been aimed elsewhere.

I had been filling her in with everything I knew - both about myself and the experiment the government was conducting. She was more shocked about the life I was leading before putting myself forward for this experiment. The memory of my failed (and embarrassing) suicide attempt had only just come back to me now I was talking about my past life. No wonder I have such strong opinions about taking my own life now. It was something I had tried to do beforehand.

"Guess I have father issues," I said - trying to make light of the situation. Crappy relationship with my real father and a dire one with my fake one too.

"So what happens now then?" she asked.

I shrugged.

"Do you think there is a way of getting our memories back? The money you mentioned - do you think that's real? Think we will get any of it? Like some form of compensation?"

I didn't reply. I didn't really know what to say to her. What I did know - though - was that there was very, very little chance of us getting any money, let alone compensation. There was also little chance of us getting out of here alive. They couldn't afford to let us go. They couldn't risk us telling anyone of what we had been through. And there was also the fact that we'd killed people. People whom we then ended up eating... If we were spotted leaving the compound - there was definitely no way they would be letting us go. I didn't say anything to Mother but I doubt Father has gotten very far.

"What are you thinking?" Mother asked.

"Guess I am thinking the same as you," I said. "Wondering what does happen next..."

My mind kept thinking about the possibility of them letting us leave this godforsaken shit-hole. The chances of them letting us go about our lives - as though none of this ever happened is extremely remote. I knew that. I wondered whether she knew it, deep down, too. Sure - it looks as though the compound I found was out of action but there would be more people to come and fill the empty offices and there'd be more people to come and run the fucked up tests. They wouldn't just leave it unmanned. For all I know - it's already running with a full complement of staff again. I also presume that it is the only way out of here - a way out which would be heavily monitored watching for people such as us leaving. I looked at Mother via the window's reflection. I can't leave with her. She will only slow me down. She will only get in the way. I need to do as Father did and break free. If I am to survive it is the best way. I know that now. It's painfully obvious the more I think about it. It slowly started to dawn on me - what I needed to do.

"We should try and get some sleep," I told her.

She stood up, "Can see what is on offer upstairs. Never know," she continued as her stomach rumbled, "there might be some food up there that someone stashed..."

"There's nothing up there," I said. "Only death."

I had earlier explained that it hadn't been the first time I had been to this house. I had told her what I found - lying in the bed upstairs. She wasn't shocked. I think she can't be shocked anymore. I know I am slowly getting desensitised to things with the more I see and live this nightmare.

"Our best bet," I told her, "is to stay in here. Leave the settee against the door just in case anything else finds the house…"

"You're expecting more of the Infected?"

Infected, soldiers, Father… Need to be prepared for anything.

"I guess it's going to be a long night," Mother said.

"You can take the settee," I told her. "I'll take the floor."

"There's probably room for two?"

"It's fine."

I walked to the corner of the room and squatted onto the floor with my back leaning on the wall. I was watching Mother as she puffed up the padding on the sofa. The way I saw it, I had two options as to how to handle her. One option, I could do as Father did and just leave during the middle of the night. The second option isn't as pretty… This second option… Part of me felt sick. Part of me felt excited.

Mother laid down and pushed herself back into the padding. She patted the slim space in front of her. I knew I was skinny but - yeah - there was no way I was going to fit on there.

"Plenty of room," she said.

I shook my head, "It's fine. I'm good here."

"Might get cold. Should cuddle up."

She winked at me. I knew what she was insinuating; that look of lust in her eyes again.

I don't like the idea of just leaving her here. It doesn't seem right. Leaving her here - alone - she is as good as dead. If not from starvation but she'll stumble into one of those things - the infected - and that will be that. She deserves more than that. The second option I am presented with is definitely the fairest.

BEFORE

Breaking Her Heart

"What have you been saying to your mother?" Dad pushed his way into my flat.

"What?"

"You've been telling her that you're not happy here?"

"I don't remember. Maybe. I might have said something."

"She says you did say something. I have no reason to doubt her. So - question begs to be asked - are you trying to cause trouble? Are you trying to rock the boat?"

"What? No. Look, I might have said something, if I did… I was just mouthing off. I wasn't trying to make things awkward for anyone. I wasn't trying to get her to talk you into letting me back home." I laughed. "You really think I want to come back to living with you?"

"I beg your pardon?"

"You're an asshole. You did me a favour, kicking me out of the house… Forcing me to this shit-hole. Sure this isn't the best of places but… I choose this over living under the same roof as you."

"Yeah?"

"Yeah. Now get the fuck out of my flat."

Dad smiled. I wasn't sure why. Maybe because I had stood up to him? Maybe he actually respected that? Usually I (and other people) do whatever he says. What he says goes. Well enough is enough. He always said I had to listen to him - even respect him - when living under his roof. Well this is my roof now.

"Let's not forget who is paying this month's rent. So - technically - this is my flat."

"Just leave."

Still smiling he leaned close to me and said, "I'll do you a deal…"

"What?"

"I will get out of your flat. I won't come back either. Ever. How does that sound? Good?"

I nodded.

"In return - you stay out of my house. For good."

"You want me to stay away from your house? What if mum invites me round for dinner?"

"She can cook for you here. I stay out of your place, you stay out of mine. Think you can do that?"

"Not a problem."

"Of course - if your mum asks - this is just as much your idea as it was mine. If she thinks it was just me… Well…"

"Yeah, I get it, you don't want to be the bad guy."

"No. Not at all."

"No?"

"If she thinks it is a mutual decision - she won't be as upset. I just don't want your mother hurt..."

⋏

NOW

The Second Option

I suppose there were three options presented to me. The first one - already mentioned - was to just leave her here during the dead of the night. Her chance of survival would be practically nil. Another option would be to take her with me but - yeah - that wouldn't really work. She would slow me down. I might need to sneak around undistracted. Can't have her slowing me down. Especially if she believes there is a chance these people - if they are out there - will just let us leave and go back to our old lives (and with compensation at that). Three options but only one that was realistic.

She had to go.

"What is it?" Mother asked.

I had been looking at her as I weighed up the options - completely oblivious to the fact she was staring right back at me.

"Just day-dreaming," I said.

I broke eye-contact.

"Oh yeah? Sounds intriguing."

She raised an eyebrow. I knew what was on her mind. Just as Sister had been - this woman was insatiable. Wonder if this is anything to do with what is in the water. Not only does the water help keep memories at bay but also - increases sexual libido. I don't know. She twisted her body up from the settee and sat up. She patted the cushion next to where she was sitting and beckoned me over.

"Come here," she purred.

I hesitated for a split second before going over to her. I didn't sit next to her. When I was standing in front of her I bent down and forced her legs apart so that I could get between them. She laughed. I pushed her back on the settee. She was breathing heavily as though getting turned on by the rougher treatment. I have a feeling she is about to be surprised. I leaned close to her face and kissed her. A small peck first before putting my tongue inside of her mouth. She responded positively. A quick thought flashed through my mind stating that I didn't have to do this but I do. I don't have a choice. The thought dissipated promptly.

Sorry, Mother.

I put my hands on her throat and moved my head away from hers. Her eyes were fixed upon mine. A smile on her face, a twinkle in her eye.

"I'm so wet for you," she sighed.

I smiled.

I squeezed her neck with my hands. Despite my intentions - she didn't seem to register the danger she was in as I continued crushing her windpipes. I felt her hand reach down for my crotch. She thinks it's a game. Something kinky to help bring her to another orgasm... I squeezed tighter as she wrapped her legs around my waist and - with them - pulled my body close to hers. Her skin was starting to flush from where I'd trapped the blood. Any second now, she's going to start to panic. Can't let go, though. Need to keep squeezing until she passes out. More than that - need to keep squeezing even after she is unconscious.

Her eyes widened. Her hand moved from my crotch up to my own hands. She tapped on my hands first - a sign telling me to get off a little. Let her have some air. Sorry, Mother, not today. Today we go all the way. The tapping changed to a frantic clawing. Her eyes staring directly into mine still - all wide and scared... They're starting to roll in the socket... Towards the back... Mostly see the whites of them now. The noises coming from her mouth, as she continued to gag, were fucked up. Can't be much longer now. Must be nearly there. Her body was writhing around - trying to push me off - but I pressed down with as much weight as I could. Come on, Mother, just go to sleep... Her head rolled to the side and her body stopped writhing, her hands stopped clawing at mine... I didn't remove my hands though. Needed to be sure she was gone.

Another minute went by and I slowly released my hands from her (bruised) neck. She didn't open her eyes, nor did she turn her head. I felt for a pulse. She was gone. I sat there a moment, unsure of what I was feeling. I had killed her - my once upon a time Mother - I should have felt sad. Maybe even a little bad for what I had done? But... I felt my crotch through my jeans. Definitely an erection present. Is that from where she was touching me through my jeans as I choked her; whilst she thought it were still all fun and games? Or is it from the act of taking her life? I tried to dismiss the idea of being turned on by her death but I struggled to. I touched my crotch and felt my cock twitch - as though it were trying to reach up to encourage my hand to wrap its fingers around it and gently wank it into a second orgasm. So soon after the first? Not even sure if I have that in me. Sure I'm young but... Lack of food equals a distinct lack of energy. Does feel good though, touching it. I continued to caress myself through the fabric of both jeans and shorts as I looked down to the gusset area of Mother's leggings. I leaned down and breathed in her scent. I pressed my face against where her vagina would be - on the other side of the cotton. Rubbing myself faster now without even realising I had changed both pace and general method of touch. Whereas a second ago I was touching myself with an open palm - now my fingers were trying to grip my cock despite the layers of clothes between them (and my ever growing hard-on).

I grabbed Mother's leggings and gave them a sharp tug down her legs. Both leggings and knickers came down with ease as the top half of her body slumped to the side. I tossed the items of clothing to the side and put my face back against her vagina - breathing in her scent whilst it was both still warm and fresh (as fresh as it could be considering the lack of soap). My hand was back around my penis, wanking it hard and fast and I gingerly poked my tongue from mouth to cunt. A bitter taste as it touched her lips. A few licks and I knew - from doing the same to Sister - that I'd soon lose the taste as the grime was washed away with my own saliva.

Part of my brain was screaming at me; asking what the hell I was doing. There was another part though which was screaming something else. It was telling me to stop licking and start fucking; take the tongue from her pussy and replace it with my hard-on. Fuck her good one last time, whilst there was still some warmth to be obtained and some juices to seep from within. You have one last time before you need to leave the house, the little voice kept saying, you need to make it a good one. For all you know, this could be the last person you get to fuck.

Guess which voice I listened to?

CHAPTER 8

BEFORE

A Mother's Love

Mum had come to visit me. She looked pale. She looked as though she'd been crying. I didn't say anything to her about her appearance. I didn't question her. I just figured that - if she wanted to talk about it - she would do so when she was good and ready. Besides which, it was a day after dad had told me I wasn't welcome around their house anymore, I had an inkling as to what was bothering her.

"How are you?" she asked.

I hadn't told her about my funny five minutes on the chair a few days ago; the rather pathetic attempt at suicide as though it were going to cure all of my problems. She probably would have wanted to know about something like that. She'd probably have wanted to help me - especially if I was suffering in any way, shape or form. I just didn't want to upset her - and I knew it would do exactly that.

"I'm good, thank you."

We were in the kitchen. I had filled the kettle with water from the tap and was waiting for it to boil. She was lucky, I hadn't been expecting any visitors and hadn't gone out for any shopping. Only just had enough milk left for a cup of tea each.

"I wasn't expecting you," I told her.

"Not interrupting, am I?" she asked.

I shook my head.

"It's nice to see you."

She smiled. The kettle clicked and I lifted it from its base and poured out two full cups of boiling water into the mugs I'd previously fetched from the cupboard.

"Your dad spoke to me," she said.

"Oh?"

"He told me you two were taking a little time apart from each other?"

I wondered whether he would even bother saying anything to her or whether it would have been down to me to find excuses not to go and visit them. Clearly he at least had the balls to say something. Well done, him. A little time apart from each other though? Was that the best he could come up with? So vague. How long was a little time? A week? Two weeks? Indefinite?

"That's right," I told her in the hope she'd carry on talking and fill in the blanks as to what he'd said to her.

"How do you feel about that?" she asked.

"I'm okay."

"Really?"

"You know things have been… strained between us for a while now."

"Well, yes."

"So, the way I see it, this could do us some good."

She smiled but I knew she wasn't happy. A rogue tear dropping from her right eye gave her away. She felt it on her cheek and wiped it away with the back of her hand. Was I to mention it? Couldn't ignore it.

"It's okay," I told her, "things will go back to normal soon enough. If anything - things will be better than they have been for a while. You watch. I'll find a decent job, I'll make something of myself and - maybe - I'll pay him back the money I owe him. Soon enough we'll be talking again. And more than that, he'll be proud of what I have achieved."

I could smell the bullshit leaking from my mouth. Even when I had had a job, even when I had had a lovely girlfriend (who dad got on with), even when I had been paying my way… He still hardly had had any time for me. There was a man - if ever one existed - who wasn't meant to have children. He was too selfish for them. He wanted to live his life with the woman he married and anything else… That just ruined what he'd planned.

"You're sure you're okay?" she asked again.

I nodded.

"I'm fine. I promise."

I reached over to her and gave her a hug as though to reiterate that everything between us was cool. Everything between us - mum and I - was cool. Nothing would change that. We didn't really say it to each other as we didn't feel the need to but I loved her and she loved me. I gave her a squeeze.

"I love you," I whispered.

"I love you too," she answered.

Sometimes it doesn't hurt to say it.

NOW

Losing It

I was kneeling on the floor next to Mother's body. My semen was dripping from her vagina, down onto the settee where her body rested. I had ejaculated but it wasn't the same sensation I was used to feeling when I'd cum all those times before. It felt… I don't know… It just wasn't the same. Despite the amount of sperm trickling from her - it felt as though it had been empty.

I looked up to her pale face. Her head was still to the side, eyes still to the back of her head.

"Get up," I told her.

She didn't move.

"Mum, get up! Stop messing around! Wake up!"

She didn't move.

I screamed out loud in the hope she'd suddenly blink and look at me, maybe even smile and tell me that she loved me, as she had when we were in the flat together sharing a cup of hot tea.

"Please, mum, stop being silly. Wake up. You're scaring me…"

I didn't want her dead. I'd acted hastily. I'd been stupid. I wanted her with me. I wanted to leave this house with her. I wanted us to go back to our old life together. Just the two of us. We've got rid of Father. We'd got rid of Sister. It would just be the two of us… Mum and I. I shook my head. What am I doing? She's not my mum. She wasn't my mum. The woman here and the woman in my flat - whenever that memory was from - they're not the same person. They're not. They're different. One is real - the one in the flat. This whore… This cunt… She is an imposter. She deserved to die. Just as Sister had deserved to die and Father too… Where ever he is… He deserves to die too. I shook my head again. No. They don't deserve to die. They didn't deserve to die. None of us deserved this. We deserved to live our lives - not in here but out there in the real world… Before this shitty experiment… None of this should have happened.

I screamed again.

My head was hurting. Banging. An ache that made me feel as though it were likely to explode in brain and skull fragments. I can't do this. I need to get out of here. I need to get away from all of this. I need to…

I need to die. Just as Sister needed to die, just as Mother needed to die - and Father. I should kill myself… I should…

No.

I can't.

I've been here before. I can't do it.

I need to go home. I need my mum. My dad, even. I need them both. They'll be able to help me through this. They'll be able to help me move on. They'll be able to help me forget the terrible things I've been forced to do in the name of science… No…

I need…

I need food…

Yes, food. I need to eat. The hunger driving me to distraction. Need to eat something. Fillet steak. Nom nom nom. Eyes cast back to Mother's body. No longer a sex toy, no longer a human… Now just a piece of meat. Fillet steak. Blue. Just the way I like it. Need to eat. Need to keep this hunger at bay…

I lunged forward, mouth open, and sunk my teeth into her fleshly thigh. I clamped my mouth shut and pulled away with a huge chunk of flesh between teeth. The taste. Oh God the taste. How I missed it. Fillet steak. That's what it is. I chewed down hard. Had to. Only way I could get it into smaller pieces. Have to chew hard. Fillet steak.

When it was small enough, I swallowed it down. My stomach instantly started to gurgle. No doubt it was gurgles of appreciation. Not much meat on a kitten and that was the last thing I forced down.

I leaned down and took another bite from her thigh and another piece of flesh from her leg. As I chewed it and swallowed it down, I immediately started to feel better about what was happening. Not the fact that I was in this situation in the first place - nothing will make me feel good about that - but rather where I should go next. I knew, now, that I needed to go home. I needed to go back to mum and dad. I needed them to help me move forward from this shitty set of circumstances. Dad? What am I talking about? I don't need him to move forward from this. I just need mum.

Swallow.

Bite.

Chew.

Wipe mouth with back of hand.

Mum always had a way of making things seem better. Whenever I had a problem, I knew I could go to her and we would talk it through until I felt better about it and had a clear idea in my head as to how best to tackle the issue until it was one hundred percent resolved. She'll be able to help me get through this. I know she will.

Swallow.

Gag.

Bite.

Chew.

Pause.

I just need to make it to where she lives. Or where I had lived. No. Wait. Can't go back there. Even if I can escape this Hell-hole - even if I can make it back to where I once lived - they'd be looking for me there; the assholes who set this place up. As I keep saying, they won't want me out there in the real world. They have seen what I have become. They know what I am; a cannibal, a murderer, a demon. They'll want me confined to a cage for life, or even put down like a rabid animal. They can't risk me out there hurting people or telling them my story. Wait. They'd know about my parents too. I must have told them about mum and dad. I must have said something to them. Did they ask for Next of Kin on the form? I'm sure they did. Not one hundred percent positive. I can't be one hundred percent sure. But... Can't remember the last time I filled in a form which didn't ask for such details. They'd look for me there too... They'd come and find me and they'd find mum. Maybe even dad. They'd find us and put us all down with a bullet to the back of the skull. Would they though? I mean, would they really? Or have I just seen one too many films? I was unemployed. I remember that much. Did I waste away my days watching movies? Is that why my imagination is so active?

I spat the Fillet Steak out and screamed a roar of frustration.

My head is a mess.

Everything is a mess.

I just need to get home. I need to be with my mum.

I need her help.

A

BEFORE

What She is There For

I watched from the top of the stairs as she walked out of my life. I wanted to call out to her, sure I did, but she had made it very clear that she no longer wanted to be with me. Mum was standing by the front door; a sympathetic look on her face. Not just for me but for my girlfriend (my ex-girlfriend) too. Break-ups were never fun and it was hard to put the blame solely on one person. Don't get me wrong, this was all her fault. She was the one who left me. She was the one who no longer wanted to be with me. The one who didn't love me. I wanted to be with her. I would have done anything to keep hold of her so - yes - in this instance it was all her own doing. But mum never judged people. She felt sorry for the pair of us because it was never nice for either party when a relationship crumbled. It wasn't nice for the person having their heart ripped out and stamped on (that would be me) and it wasn't nice for the person who had to put someone else through that pain.

Mum opened the door and said goodbye to my ex. My ex - a sheepish look on her face - said goodbye too as mum closed the door - blocking my vision from seeing my ex head off down the driveway and out of my life. I sat on the top stair. I felt completely numb. Maybe a little bit sick even? Mum walked to the bottom of the stairs and looked up at me with that same sympathetic look she'd given my ex.

"You heard then?" I asked her.

"Hard not to. There was a lot of shouting," she said.

I felt embarrassed. Not just because I was so worthless that I had been dumped but because mum had heard us. No doubt she heard me begging for my relationship to have another chance. I must have sounded pathetic.

"Are you okay?" mum asked.

I didn't answer. In the great scheme of things - yes - I was okay but, in the short of it, no I wasn't okay. I was anything but okay. I felt as though my heart had literally been pulled from my rib-cage and stamped on several times over. I felt as though I were a worthless, undesirable piece of shit. I felt... I felt horrible. I also felt anger. Anger? Yes. Anger. I felt angry that this whore had dared to leave me. Leave me? How could she? She was lucky to have me in the first place. She'll realise that over the next few days. She will realise and she will come running back to me.

"You know what you need? Hot chocolate. I even have those little pieces of marshmallow that you like," she said.

I couldn't help but smile. The thought of hot chocolate didn't make me feel better, it didn't fix anything. I smiled because the hot chocolate was something mum always made for me when I wasn't at my best. At school, I had fallen over and scuffed my entire knee... Took loads of skin off. Mum was there, when I limped home, hot chocolate in hand. Years later I had an operation for my appendix. When I got home from the hospital - first thing mum did after getting me set up on the sofa with a pile of movies... Yep - a nice hot chocolate with extra marshmallow pieces. The drink never fixed things. It simply let me know that - whatever I was going through - mum was there for me. My own little guardian angel.

"I'd like that," I told her.

She smiled and walked down the hallway, back towards the kitchen where she could prepare my drink. I didn't move. I just sat there, on the top stair, staring at the front door wondering if there'd be a little knock at it… Wondering if she was going to come back, with her tail between her legs.

Please come back.

λ

NOW

A Lonely Walk

I could barely see anything as I stumbled my way through the woods. It was foolish of me to leave the relative comfort of the house but I felt as though I had to make a move sooner rather than later. Something inside of me screaming for me to get back to where mum lived. My mind asking whether she was even aware I had left the flat in order to take part in this fucked up experiment.

The longer I had sat in the house, thinking about leaving, the more I had persuaded myself that it was the right thing to do. If I can't see out here, my brain told me, then those infected bastards won't be able to see me either. We'd both be blind. Of course - now I was out here - my brain was wondering whether they had super vision or anything like that? After all - it was clear these things were strong. My brain further explained that it would make sense if all of their senses were heightened. After all - if it were an experiment then there'd be a good chance they would want all the side effects to be positive? Something - I was guessing - to administer to their soldiers before sending them overseas to fight in whatever pointless battle they had enrolled them in. Obviously the serum wasn't up to scratch yet - hence letting the infected bastards loose into the compound so as to munch on each other (and us). All of this was just guess work. I didn't know what was going through their mind when they engineered this shit. Was it for good or was it for evil? I'll never know. But - regardless - I just wish my brain would shut the fuck up about it. It's creepy enough out here without worrying about running into some super soldier.

Not sure how long I had been walking for now. It seemed like forever but I was almost certain I had made little to no headway. I had come away from the main road (if you could call it a road) so as to disappear amongst the trees and bushes and progress was painfully slow due to walking, using my hands as my eyes. I was also doing a weird little shuffle with my feet. It seemed like the sensible thing to do - slide my feet over the dirt and gravel beneath me so as to make it less of a trip hazard.

I froze.

What was that?

Heard something.

Sounded like a twig snapping a little way away from me in the distance. I held my breath as I waited for another tell-tale sound that would further suggest something was close to me. There was nothing. Had they heard me as I had heard them? Are they standing out there - a few feet away from me - waiting to hear if I make a move myself? I caught my tongue when I realised I was on the verge of calling out as to whether anyone was there, or not. If they are there, I don't want them knowing I am here. I want them to miss me. No confrontation. Especially with one of those things. They're too strong. Reminds me…

I reached under my shirt and pulled a knife from where I had it tucked under my belt. I had taken it from the kitchen before leaving the house for this very situation. I gripped the handle tight in my hands as I prepared myself to lunge for whatever would possibly be coming from the shadow. Please be nothing, please be nothing - I kept mentally telling myself over and over again. I slowly exhaled before taking another breath, as quietly as I could. Another snap from what must have been a few feet away. There is something there. Something or someone?

"WHERE THE FUCK ARE YOU?" a voice called out from the side.

Who the hell was that?

Another snap from in front of me, more frequent this time, as if someone was moving away from me, fumbling their way through the bushes back towards the sound of where the other voice had come from.

"I told you to go before we left," the first voice said.

"Yeah, yeah, whatever… Give me my gun."

"Here."

Gun? What? Must be military. No one else would have any reason to have a gun out here. That can't be part of the experiment. No way. Has to be part of the cleaning-up of the experiment.

"Where the fuck is this property anyway?" the first voice asked.

I crouched down on the off-chance I was visible. Surrounded by so much black and shrubbery I was sure I wasn't but it was better to be safe than sorry. Especially given the fact they have guns. Fucking guns?

"There's one a little further down the road where they could be holding up or the house where they were staying is another mile away."

"We should have a team for this."

"Relax. The occupants of the first house took their own lives so they're dealt with and there are - potentially - only three left of the second group. You want to prove yourself for that promotion, or what?"

"Yeah because I'm sure they'll be pleased we didn't wait for morning as instructed and decided to go it alone. Is that a promotion for showing initiative and getting the job done or is it a court marshal for disobeying direct orders?"

"They have enough to deal with back at the offices. They'll be pleased we sorted it."

"Well if they're not - this was your fucking idea."

"Fuck you…"

"Come on, let's just get this done. Fucking creepy out here."

The footsteps were getting further away as they headed back towards the house I had just come from. I'd heard enough to warn me that - back where the sheds were and offices etc - there was a team there on clean-up duties (me being what needed cleaning up) and I had learned that Father was no longer something to be fearful of bumping into. Clearly he had been found. The two dimwits in the dark said there were three of us left. That would be Sister, Mother and I, suggesting Father was gone. Part of me wondered whether he'd been imprisoned or simply shot. A bigger part of me didn't give a fuck. Just so long as he is gone, that's fine by me. There was more though… And it was far more alarming than the immediate danger I was in from meandering soldiers in the dark…

They wanted me dead - or caught - and, unless I gave them something else to focus their energy on, I wouldn't be safe no matter where I hid. More than that - mum and dad might not be safe. Fuck dad but… I don't want mum in danger.

Chapter 9

Dear Dad

Dad and I hadn't spoken for weeks now. We hadn't even seen each other. I thought I would have felt a little sad about this because - when all was said and done - he was my blood. He was my family. He was my dad. I felt nothing though... Well, almost nothing. There was one thing in my mind. It wasn't even buried at the back under old memories. It was right there - right in the forefront of my mind. A single, loud thought; I wished he were dead.

I knew it would break mum's heart - and for that I felt bad - but I couldn't help myself. The fact he was out there, living his life without a care in the world despite the pain he caused people (he was an asshole to everyone), it just made me feel sick. Why should he get away with being an asshole? Why should everyone else suffer because he was still breathing air as opposed to burning in hell? Fuck him. He deserved to die.

NOW

Father, Sweet Father

From where I was standing in the bushes, I could see the car Father had taken from us when he'd stormed from the house. I could also see that it wasn't empty. All the doors were closed and - at a glance - everything looked normal. But if you strained your eyes, in the poor lighting conditions, and actually looked properly you would see that nothing was normal about the way the car was parked up by the smashed gates of the compound. Little light, from the spotlights on the wall close to the car, showed a shape in the driver's seat - slumped forward. I didn't need to go closer to the car. I didn't need more light. I could tell that it was Father. They must have heard the car coming. They must have come to the front of the compound, guns raised, and opened fire without question. Further straining of the eyes and I could see bullet-holes in the metalwork of the car. They hadn't accidentally let a shot off which just happened to hit Father - killing him. They had opened fire with multiple rounds. He wouldn't have stood a chance. More to the point, we wouldn't have stood a chance.

Had it not been for Sister running from the car… Had it not been for Father taking the car from us and abandoning us… We would be in there, rotting away with his corpse right now… I felt sick at the thought of how much these people wanted us dead. They wanted us alive for the test and now that was over, they wanted us dead. To know human life was so worthless to them was scary. They could do it to us - fuck us over - so they could fuck others over too.

My thoughts raced back to the men I'd stumbled across within the woods; two assholes with guns, looking for Sister, Mother and I in order to end our lives. These people wanted us dead and would stop at nothing. Soon they would come back with the news that Mother and Sister were both dead but that I was still out there, on the run. A bigger team would sweep the premises and the woodlands - of that I am sure - but it will only be a matter of time before they head off into the outside world to try and find me.

I need to do something to take their mind off me. I need to create a bigger problem for them to contend with; something so big that they'd be so preoccupied with whatever it is that I could go on about my life with my mum. My real mum.

There's only one thing I could think of - which might be of some use to me in this current predicament… And that was the infected. Whatever it was they were trying to achieve with the shit they were putting into people - whether the purpose was to be used for good, or bad… Whatever it was… It was contagious (if bitten) and it was deadly. If there was an outbreak of that out in the real world… That… That might just give them enough to worry about that they'd leave me be.

I cast my eyes down the length of the wall. Not too far away I could see the tree I must have used the first time, to get over the wall; a tall tree that grew near the wall - offering a sturdy branch to, once again, help me over it. Better still - it was in a relatively dark area. None of these damned spotlights.

A quick look around to make sure I wasn't seen by anyone, or close enough to accidentally raise an alarm when I made my move, and I hurried over to the tree as quietly as I could. Once at the tree, I wasted no time in getting up onto the branch that was level with the wall. Of all the trees out here, I do believe I have found the exact same tree I climbed the first time I stumbled upon the wall and that - once again - it was going to take a leap (of faith) to get from the branch onto the top of wall. Please God don't let me slam my gut into the ledge again like last time. Never mind the fact it hurt - last time I had to do this, I nearly slipped back on the wrong side of the wall...

I didn't go for the jump immediately, when I did get to the necessary branch. I waited there, looking around - specially at what I could see over the wall. It was still dark but I knew there was a chance the sun would start to come up soon. Felt as though I had walked for hours and hours and it can't stay night all the time. Sadly. As long as it's dark now though, that's all that matters. Keep telling yourself that. It's dark now. It's dark now. Make your move. Get over the wall and on your way to freedom. Make it happen.

I took a deep breath and threw myself at the top of the wall. This time I caught it just right and didn't wind myself. Getting good at this. Just as I had done so before, I pulled my body up and over so that I was lying on the top of the thick breeze-blocked structure. Out of breath. Tired. Should have eaten more of Mother before coming out. Should have got my strength up. This is no time to start struggling with energy levels. No time at all.

I twisted my head to the side (at the operations down below) and felt a heavy sinking feeling as I realised how many people were milling around - walking into and out of the various cabins dotted around the place. From where I was waiting, I could see that many of the cabins were raised from the floor by small stilts. A couple of stairs leading up to the doors. There wasn't a massive gap under the buildings but there was enough of a gap there for me to crawl under. I was sure of it. All I had to do was make it down to the first cabin and get under it and then - with patience - I could work my way towards the compound's exit point. A simple enough plan until I remembered what happened the last time I tried to get down from the wall. I had gotten down successfully but somewhat cocked the landing up and knocked myself clean out. If I do that this time - I'm dead. No pressure then.

A gunshot rang out in the distance and made me jump out of my skin. The crack ripped through the air from beyond the wall - back in the experiment's zone. Remembering that there were multiple zones with multiple people - such as myself - I couldn't help but wonder whether the military folk had stumbled into one of the normal test subjects or whether they'd put one of the Infected out of their misery. A second and third gunshot echoed up to where I laid flat. I'm guessing it was one of the normal subjects. Poor bastards. That's what waits for me, though, if I don't get down from here soon. A bullet.

They say somewhere in the world there is a bullet with your name on it. Not sure who 'they' are exactly but it is definitely a saying. If there is a bullet out there with the name John Burley on it... Well I don't want to catch it just yet. I sat up, on the wall, and quickly dangled my feet over the edge (the side with the cabins). A little bit of manoeuvring and I was soon facing the wooded area but dangling over the other side of the wall in an effort to lower myself down to the ground. Without thinking - I let go of the wall and dropped down. I landed hard on my feet and fell backwards onto my arse. Definitely painful but also better than landing face first like last time.

Voices close to me. Calm voices. Not disturbed. Not in a state of alarm.

I quickly scrambled over to the first cabin and dragged my tired (and bruised) body underneath it. It was a tight squeeze but I'd rather that than be out in the open like a sitting duck. Just need to edge my way to the other side and - when the coast is clear - roll across to the next cabin. Keep doing that until I am close to the exit point or another set of woods which might lead me back to civilisation.

Voices in the building above me.

"You see that son of a bitch in the car?"

"Sure did..."

"Thought he was never going to go down. Never seen someone take so many bullets…"

"When in doubt, always go for the headshot."

The way they were talking - as though killing Father (I presume it was him they were talking about) was acceptable - made me feel sick. Not just that. I felt a rage brewing within me. I'd love nothing more than to rush the cabin and tear them limb from limb; hurt them like I hurt that technician… That cunt I found hiding away… What was his name… Bray? Michael Bray. I want to hurt these assholes just as I hurt him.

"You will get more practise, I'm sure. Tomorrow we clear out the rest of the zones."

I carefully crawled across to the far side of the cabin. Once there, a quick look to my right pin-pointed the next one. Just as suspected, it also had a crawl space that I could utilise. Just as well really. Don't think I fancy running across an open space with a bunch of soldiers all looking for a target to practice their sharp-shooting skills upon.

Satisfied the coast was clear, I rolled from underneath the cabin and continued to roll until I was underneath the next. No sense getting up and running across. Far easier just to keep rolling.

I heard someone above me. They were screaming to be let out. I didn't know who it was. Going with how they handled Father, they're clearly not into taking prisoners at the moment which suggests it is someone waiting to be infected with the shit they have manufactured but that makes no sense either. If they're clearing the areas out - why have more people ready and waiting to be turned into just another government fuck up? Not my problem. I crawled to the middle of the space and froze. Someone was standing in front of me, next to the steps leading to the cabin's entrance. They hadn't seen me - obviously - but I didn't want to make any noise which might alert them to my presence. Trapped rat down here.

"Shit…" the person muttered.

A set of keys dropped to the floor next to his feet; clearly dropped. Before the person bent down to pick them up, he placed a metal canister on the floor next to his feet. He then bent down and scooped up the keys. He then lifted the canister back out of my eye-line and continued on up the steps. I heard the keys enter the lock and the door open. He stepped from stair to wooden floor of the cabin. The door slammed shut.

The canister told me everything I needed to know about what was going on in that room. A label on it suggesting it was both highly toxic and highly flammable. Clearly the person in there - calling out for freedom - was yet another test subject. Could have sworn Michael Bray - the lab rat I had found hiding in one of the many cabins... I could have sworn he said there was no 'testing' carried out here. There was a good chance my memory didn't serve me correctly - what with all I have been through - but I felt sure he said the experiments were carried out elsewhere and the people - infected - were merely released here. But then, I didn't know Bray other than the fact he was a lab rat for the assholes running this place. What reason did he have to tell me the truth? Could have been a lie in an effort to save himself. It wouldn't surprise me. I think it's fair to say nothing will surprise me again.

I continued my escape bid and made my way to the cabin edge. I stayed there long enough to let two sets of feet walk on by and around the corner. Satisfied they were gone, I rolled across to the next cabin; an idea formulating in my mind.

All the way here I was thinking about setting off an explosion. I wasn't sure exactly how my plan would work other than the fact there had to be flammable liquids around here; or something highly combustible at least. But - thinking about it now - maybe that isn't the best way to get them off my back. After all, it wouldn't take them long to sort out an explosion and (potential) resulting fire caused by it. And it certainly wouldn't take everyone to deal with it. But...

Those canisters.

If I could find where they were kept and maybe undo the tops of them, or maybe cause an explosion with those and release some of that shit into the atmosphere... Maybe that would give me room to breathe? Surely if enough of it is released I'd be able to infect at least some of the fuckers milling around the place? They would then attack some of the other soldiers and lab geeks roaming around and they - in turn - would become infected; just like Sister was. I'm sure they'd be able to get it under control after a while but not until I am well and truly clear of any danger and - by then - they'd be more worried about stopping that from happening again than trying to find one quiet person... And I would be quiet. I'd slip off the radar. Go back to mum and just keep my head down. Let her help me get over this whole fucked up experience. Would I even tell her? I'd have to. She'd see something is wrong. I couldn't hide it from her. Not this. She's too clever.

A series of thuds came from the cabin I'd just rolled away from, making me jump. It sounded as though someone was being thrown around in there, or at least throwing themselves against the side of the building. I didn't dare move as I knew the loud bangs would attract attention from elsewhere too. And I was right. The people who'd only just walked on by appeared again; hurried footsteps towards the other cabin. The door opened before they got there and the man who'd dropped the keys came staggering out; a mask on his face.

"What the fuck is going on in there?" one of the other men asked.

The masked man slammed the door shut and locked it with the keys he pulled from his pocket.

"He turned immediately!" he shouted when he took the mask off. "I literally held the mask up to his face and turned the gas on and he fucking turned... Blink of an eye. I only just managed to get the cage shut so I could get away from him... He broke the chains and everything!" the man continued. "They've changed the formula! They must have! I didn't even use the whole dosage."

"Wait - what? Tell me you closed the valve on the canister?"

"Of course I did. Jesus. What do you take me for?"

"Is he secure?" the second man butted in.

The (once) masked man ignored the second man's comment, "We need to find a new way to administer this stuff. If we're going to get no time delay between giving them a sniff and them changing, it's far too dangerous to do it this way. He could have fucking killed me. Where's Dr. Plouffe?" he asked.

"You really want to bother her because you got scared?"

"It's dangerous. It's an accident waiting to happen. They have changed something in those canisters and made it more potent. They can't do that without warning us first. Someone has to say something..."

"Maybe they did it on purpose? Maybe they're looking for a way of killing all you lab rats?" the second soldier laughed.

"Fuck you," the (once) masked man stormed away in the opposite direction.

"Come on," the second man turned to the first, "we should check he really is secure in there."

"You got the key?"

"Yeah I have a set of masters. They still not trust you with them?"

"Honestly, lose one set and they never forgive you…"

I turned away from the scene and crawled towards the middle of the cabin to ensure I was out of their line of sight. A little more of my plan coming into fruition; I get in that cabin and I get to that canister… And then I simply open the valve and get the fuck out of there. That guy - the one who took the can in there to begin with - he'll come back with this Dr. Plouffe and - done - they're both infected. They attack anyone else who decides to go in and check in on them and - hopefully - there'll be a domino effect as more and more become infected. It might not be the best plan - especially as I don't know whether simply holding my breath will stop me from becoming infected - but given the circumstances it's the best I have to offer. And if I do become one of those infected bastards… Well hopefully I will still help to spread the infection around the rest of the base camp. The way I see it, I do not really have much to lose at this point… The only real problem with the plan is that I first need to deal with the two assholes who've just gone inside and - what's more - I need to be quick about it.

A quick check around me to see if the coast was clear and I pulled myself out from underneath the cabin. I reached for my belt, where I'd put the knife, and pulled it from where it rested. I never was much of a fighter… Need to make this surprise attack count.

⅄

BEFORE

A Gentle Soul

My eye was sore. I already knew that it was going to swell up. My nose was hurting too; a shooting pain that went from tip to brain relentlessly and had been as such from the moment my classmates fist connected with it. What was the reason? Why did he lash out? I must have said something. I know I must have said something to get such a reaction but - what was it? What the hell did I do to deserve this?

Of course I retaliated. I hit back. For what it was worth. I most definitely came off worst and now - to add insult to injury - my mum had been called at her work place. Before she could take me home, she had to have a meeting with The Head.

Zero tolerance on fighting, they said.

I know I'll be facing a suspension. The other boy - he might get worse. It's not the first time he has been in The Head's office. Maybe this will be the final straw that sees him thrown from the school? I hope so. I don't want to see him again.

I looked towards The Head's secretary. Even she looked angry at me. It's strange - all of these disapproving looks... All of these private conversations in shut off rooms - all centred around me - and yet none of them bother me. None of them are causing me much room for concern. The only one that's on my mind is the conversation I'll be having with dad when he gets home from work. He's often late home. Sometimes so late I am already in bed. Sod's Law dictates that tonight is the one night he is home early though. The one night I can't escape his harsh words by pretending to be asleep.

Please God don't let him come home early.

The door to The Head's room opened and mum came out. She looked upset. A wave of guilt rushed through me. I caused that. She walked over to me and told me to get my bag (which was on the floor nestled between my feet). She was angry. More than that, she was disappointed. She hadn't even asked if I was okay yet, nor had she asked me for my side of what happened. I bent down, picked my bag up, and jumped off the chair. She thanked the secretary (for what I don't know) and headed for the door. I followed with my tail between my legs.

The drive home was more or less in silence. Mum did finally ask whether I was okay after telling me that I'd been suspended for a week. A week? That wasn't bad. It could have been worse. She looked worried, though. I guessed that was because she too was concerned with how dad was going to react to what I had done.

Eleven years old and suspended from school. Hardly something to be proud of.

Naturally the conversation with dad didn't go well (when he did finally come home). He must have been told on the phone, before getting there, because when

I went downstairs to see him - and face the music - he was standing there, in the living room, in front of the fire with his back to me. The look in his eyes when he turned around and looked at me. So many emotions right there and none of them good. Disgust, shame, anger...

By the time he finished berating me I was in floods of tears. The harsh words he used (I'm a nasty vindictive little bastard) destroyed me. He didn't even care that I wasn't the first to throw a punch. To him - the little details didn't matter. He was all about the end picture. When he finally did finish shouting, and let me go to my room, I ran up there and slammed the door. Honey, my hamster, was up and running on her wheel in the cage. I walked over to her with such hatred flowing through my veins and - before I knew what I was doing - I was shaking the cage violently.

The age old scenario; man shouts at dog, dog bites cat, cat eats mouse.

The following day, I buried my hamster whilst wondering whether I'd ever be brave enough to aim my anger at those who deserved it; the ones who made me feel bad. Mum, unaware of the true reason my hamster died, comforted me with hot chocolate, extra marshmallow.

⋏

NOW

Leak

I plunged the knife in the neck of the first soldier and pulled it out. His back was to me and he never saw his attacker. As soon as the blade was removed - a fine spray of blood pumped out, hitting the wall on the other side of the small cabin. The man clutched at his wound as he fell to the floor with a thud. The second soldier turned around in time to see my teeth coming at him. With one hand on the side of his face, I pulled him close and took a chunk from his face. The speed with which I moved, the ferocity - all he did was scream as I spat his nose to the floor. Before he had a chance to do anything else, I brought the knife up into his gut with the blade angled upwards. Again, when I pulled the blade out, he dropped to the floor next to his comrade.

I wiped my mouth clean of gore and nestled the knife under my belt once more before bending down and taking the second soldier's gun; a small pistol. I have no training with regards to fire-arms; never even had a pellet gun when I was growing up. I still figured it was better to have it on the off-chance I needed it though. Besides, as he bled out like a stuffed pig, he wasn't going to need it. Nor was his colleague who was already dead.

"Please - you have to let me out of here," a man said.

I turned my attention to the cabin. Four small cages (sitting room only) were lined against the wall. The last cage had an infected man in it - chained up like an animal. He was going mad; snarling and pulling at the restraints which kept him attached to the wall. One woman, two men in the other cages - all nervously waiting for their turn to be turned. All scared.

The canister - the very thing I came in here for - was on the floor next to the Infected bastard's cage. I reached down to the second soldier and patted down his pockets until I heard the tell-tale sounds of keys jingling in his clothes. I smiled and reached for them, pulling them out.

"Come on - what are you waiting for - let us out!"

I turned to the man shouting at me and wondered upon the crime he'd committed to find himself shackled up in this cage. Or - maybe - he was like me and innocent in all of this? I don't ask him. I'm not here to make friends. From here on in - I'm sticking only with my family.

"The keys are up there!" he told me.

He pointed behind me, to the wall. I turned and saw - hanging from a small hook - a silver key.

"Please. Look what they're doing to people. You can't just leave us here."

I walked over to the key and removed it from the hook.

"Thank you, thank you, thank you…" he said.

I walked back over to the cages and collected the canister. I took it over to the door by the exit.

"What are you doing?" the man asked.

"You'll need to be quick," I told him.

"What are you doing?" he asked again.

I threw him the small silver key and took a deep breath. He knew exactly what I was going to do and fumbled around on the floor, looking for the key. He found it and started to work the lock as best as he could from the angle he was at. I - in the meantime - turned the valve on the canister releasing a plume of green smoke into the air. I kicked the canister over and it rolled back towards the cages. The three prisoners starter to scream as I opened the door, gun in hand, and made my escape.

Outside I checked around to ensure I was alone. To my relief I was. I closed the door and hurried back over to the space under the third cabin, letting myself breathe the fresh air. By the time I got underneath the cabin, the screams had stopped. I felt no guilt. It was entirely necessary. They have their part to play.

I wasted no time in crawling to the other side of the space. Need to be quick. Need to get out of here. Need to get home to mum. Need to put this whole fucked up situation behind me once and for all. I'm coming home, mum!

Chapter 10

Broken

As I made my way from cabin to cabin - I couldn't help but get stuck on the freshly-returned memory of killing my hamster. A cruel thing to do - one for which I felt shame for what felt to be the first time. An innocent life, snatched away from me for no other reason than I was an ill-tempered asshole. Was this the person I really was? I didn't get my own way, or I got shouted at and I took my vengeance on those I felt I could hurt, as opposed to clashing with those I wanted to hurt? Was I never really a man and simply nothing more than a lowlife coward? I kept trying to turn my mind from the thought but - no matter what I did - it always returned to the same ones; I was a coward. Perhaps I deserved to be locked away in here?

I shook it from my mind again.

No.

I deserve to be at home.

If that was the person I was then I truly am sorry but that's not me anymore. I swear. I've changed. I can change. I will change. I want to change. I'll be good. If someone wrongs me, I will react accordingly to those individuals directly as opposed to venting towards those who cannot escape me. Wait. No… That would make me like him, the bully from school. Jesus - what was his name? What was it? Come on brain. Think. Why? Why do I even care what his name was? He's long gone from my life and never likely to come back. I need to know his name though. I need to remember it. If I can't remember his name, maybe the rest of the memory isn't correct either? Maybe the rest of the memory is tainted by what I've gone through since being trapped here. No. Wait. His name…

His name was Ted.

I realised I was at the last cabin. Nowhere to hide after I roll from this one. I'll be out in the open. Need to wait here for a moment, wait for someone to discover what I had done in the cabin. Go when everyone is distracted.

As I waited around, my mind drifted to thoughts of what was going on back at home. I wondered whether mum and dad even realised I had been missing. I also tried to piece together where their house was exactly. I can picture it. Interior and exterior. If I concentrate, I can even see the rest of the street too but the exact location… The exact location - at the moment - escapes me. I should be worried about that. Can hardly run off and live happy ever after with mum knowing full well that I can't recall the address properly.

Don't panic, John, you'll remember it.

Memories are slowly coming back to me. It's just a matter of time before the address just pops up, right there, in my mind too. Just a matter of time. Yes but - until then - what do I do? Where do I go? Stop worrying about it. Just head into civilisation - away from this place and stress about it then. That's all you can do.

I jumped at the sound of a shrill alarm piercing the night.

Looks like they've discovered what I've done.

I jumped again at the sound of gunfire and screams.

This is it. Time to make a run for it.

I looked around again - a final check to ensure I wasn't about to run straight into trouble. Coast is clear. More gun shots coming from the cabin, and more screams; along with panicked shouting which I couldn't quite make out. The distraction is working then. I rolled from underneath the cabin and ran towards what looked as though it could have been a security checkpoint. I took a hold of the gun in one hand and the knife in another. If it is a checkpoint - and it is manned - I'll be ready.

My heart skipped a beat as an alarm rang through the air. A shrill noise which hurt my ear-drums. I tried to ignore it as I continued to near the checkpoint. Come on, come on, nearly there… Gun raised ready to blast any-one who'd dare show their faces. The gunshots won't matter. I'm not sure what's happening back there, back at the cabin, but it's created a lot of noise and a lot of gunfire.

I reached the checkpoint and carefully looked through the small window. To my relief, the room was empty. Not sure whether it was ever manned or whether everyone was inside now, all on clean-up duty for the mess they'd cre-ated and - more specifically - the mess I had created both now and the last time I was here. Although I can't take full responsibility for things going wrong the last time I was here. Sure, I killed Bray - the lab rat - but something had already happened before I had got here. The place was a mess with bodies everywhere. What did he say it was? What did Bray say it was again? Fuck. What's going on with my memory. Old memories coming back to me slowly and little things - re-cent things - I find myself forgetting them. Can't complain. That's hope for the future. Could be there is a slim possibility of forgetting all of this ever happened. I laughed. Chances. I beat a man to death with a shovel and ate his corpse. You don't forget shit like that. I turned away from the window and froze. Something caught my eye in the tiny box room. I slowly turned back. There - on the wall - keys hanging. On the other side of the gate - where I was headed - there were a row of cars all parked up…

Could it be Lady Luck was looking down upon me once again?

I reached for the booth's silver handle and twisted it. The door opened. I went into the room and took all of the sets of keys that were hanging there. Some of them were clearly for cabins, or other buildings but some of them… Some of them were definitely for vehicles. Please be for one of the cars out there. Please…

BEFORE

An Accident

I was sitting in the house nervously waiting for dad's arrival home from the of-fice. It was already ten o'clock at night so clearly he was having a bad day and - he wasn't to know it yet - it was only going to get worse when he was to finally come in, knackered and no doubt grumpy.

I had passed my theory test over a couple of months ago. First time. The practical test though - the one meaning I could drive on the roads without anyone sitting next to me - that had taken a few times to get through. Four to be precise but today was the day. Today was the day I became a fully qualified driver. It was also the first time I'd ever been in a car accident.

I had got home full of self-confidence and a need to hit the open road. A little bit of begging and mum finally let me take her car out on the road. Her last words to me before I left were telling me to be careful. And I was careful. The car behind me wasn't so careful. As I went to pull out of a junction, I stalled the car and then - wham - they drove right up my arse. There wasn't a lot of damage but there was enough to make it obvious and necessary to fix.

Mum wasn't angry. She knew accidents happen. But we both knew dad wouldn't be as calm about it. He'd be angry at me for having the crash - even though it wasn't my fault - and he would be angry with mum for letting me go out alone, despite having a licence.

Just wished he'd hurry up and get home so we could get this over and done with. There'd be a moment of calm before the storm and then he'd start shouting. The shouting would last a few days - sometimes weeks - and then he would gradually start to calm down. That's the way it works around here. I knew it, mum knew it.

My heart skipped a beat when I heard the sound of dad's car reversing into the driveway. Funny how I could always recognise his car from the noise the engine made. A gentle ticking noise as he edged his way back, next to mum's car. A few seconds later and his engine stopped. Another few seconds went by and his car door opened and then slammed shut again.

Shit, here we go.

"It'll be fine," mum gave me (what she thought to be) a reassuring smile.

We both knew it wasn't going to be fine. We both knew he was going to be mad.

I mentally prepared myself for the telling off when I heard the front door open and then close again. This is it.

"What the hell happened to your car?" dad shouted from the hallway as he took his suit jacket off and hung it over the bannister.

"I had an accident," mum said before I had the chance to say anything, "someone ran into me in town…"

I shot mum a look. I couldn't believe she was taking the blame for it. I wanted to say something. I wanted to tell the truth. I didn't though. I just smiled back at mum who - in turn - flashed me a wink.

NOW

Highway From the Danger Zone

I slid the key into the ignition with the same amount of both fear and hope that I had the last time I managed to find myself a vehicle. Will it work? Will it have petrol? Will I make it half way down the road before a bullet shatters the back window and (more worryingly) my head? I gave it a twist and the engine fired up first time. One question answered. I turned my attention to the fuel gauge. It bounced on empty for a split second before moving up to near full. Second question answered. I put the car into first gear and slammed my foot on the accelerator hoping Lady Luck would skip the third question I'd previously worried about.

The car's back wheels spun in the mud as the car momentarily struggled for traction before getting a grip and launching the car down the muddy road which (I presumed) lead the way back to town. At the first opportunity I turned down a side road. I had no idea whether it was the right way or not, hard to tell when you don't know where you are to start off with, but - whatever - it would make it harder for them to see me and shoot at me.

Another turn and the muddied road turned to one of a more concrete base. Good.

Must be on the right path.

I kept checking in the rear-view mirror as I sped away from Hell to see if I was being followed. No headlights coming after me. No bullets flying past (or into) the car. I think I got away with it; my daring escape. I think I'm in the clear. I smiled. Guess my distraction did the job. Way to go me. Now I only had one thing on my mind… Where the hell do I live?

BEFORE

Confused

Not my bed. Not my house. Not a house? Room full of other beds - all of them filled with people I don't recognise. I don't know them. I don't think I've ever known them, it's not that I have just forgotten who they are. They are strangers. Definitely. Strangers in a strange place. White walls, white floors, white sheets on the beds (all of them).

"Hello?" I called out. "Mum?"

Always when I'm worried, always when I am concerned about something... Why do I first call for my mum? He's an asshole but surely dad would be better in a situation where you need help? He's stronger!

"Mum!" I called out again.

Well - speaking part of my brain disagrees then...

A set of double-doors opened at the far end of the room and a middle-aged woman walked in dressed in a nurses' uniform. She walked right by the other beds, all the way to the one where I was lying. She was smiling at me. This strange woman smiling at me - a smile that seemed to say 'don't worry, everything is going to be okay'. I relaxed a little.

"Do you know where you are?" she asked.

I shook my head.

"You're in hospital. You've had an accident. You hit your head."

An accident? I don't remember.

"My head hurts."

The woman put her hand on my wrist and checked my pulse.

"Do you know your name?" she asked.

I nodded.

"John."

"My name is Natalie," she said. "Is there anyone you would like for us to call?"

"My mum?"

"Do you remember the phone number?" Natalie asked.

I tried to think but my head pounded. I shook my head and - again - complained about my headache.

"That's okay," she said.

"What's your surname?" she asked. "Do you remember that?"

I thought for a moment and nodded, "Burley."

"And your address? What about that?" she asked.

"Why can't I remember?"

"You hit your head. It's quite common for a little confusion," she reassured me. "Do you know your address? Help us track down a phone number for your parents…"

NOW

The Path is Revealed

I couldn't remember the reason why I'd been in hospital but I didn't care. I remembered the conversation with the nurse. I remembered her name even - Natalie. I remembered the smell of her sweet perfume and her pretty, reassuring smile. But more than that I remembered the address I gave her.

I pressed my foot down harder on the accelerator until it was touching the floor. All I needed was a road sign, or something. Something to tell me where I was. Something to give me some bearings which would help me get home. Something other than the damned woods which currently line the sides of the road. Wherever I am, wherever we were, they wanted us kept far and away from civilisation.

It doesn't matter though. Have a nearly full tank of petrol. No one is following; all too pre-occupied at the camp area. I'm in the clear and nothing will stop me from getting home.

I'm coming, mum. I'm coming.

Soon be time to put all of this behind me.

Chapter 11

My Home

The sun had come up. A nice day. I'd put the car window down earlier - whilst I was driving in an effort to keep me awake with the cold air coming in from the outside. Now I could feel the warmth of the sun beaming down upon my skin and could hear the birds singing in the distance.

I was parked up outside mum and dad's house. I recognised the cars in the driveway. They were both home. Not for much longer though. Within the next thirty minutes, dad would be leaving for work. An hour after that and mum would be leaving for her day in the office too. Mum's car - the one I had had the accident in was parked up on the left - and dad's Mercedes SL 500 was parked up on the right. It was always that way round; mum on the left and dad always on the right. Only just dawned on me the subtext of the parking arrangements echoed their relationship; 'dad was always right'. I wonder if he realised what he was doing when he 'claimed' that space on the driveway.

I had turned the car engine off so as not to attract any unwanted attention from other people leaving their houses and that was as far as I had got. I had been driving for hours and was tired and - worse than that - the memories continued to flood back to me. Like the partial memory of being laid up in that hospital bed. When the memory first popped back to mind, during the long night, I couldn't remember what had landed me there - other than the nurse saying it had been an accident. Now - though - I remember the whole story. It hadn't been an accident. He meant to shove me. He meant to throw his weight around.

My dear dad.

I saw him with someone that wasn't mum. I questioned him about it and we got into a fight. Son of a bitch shoved me so hard that I fell backwards and banged my head on the wall behind me. Knocked me out cold. This asshole - this piece of shit - that I used to be fearful of. The man always pretended to be something special, he always pretended to be the boss; lording it up over us (and everyone else) but all this time he was nothing but a lowlife piece of shit. He used to talk of respect, when we were growing up, but he didn't give respect to anyone else. He just expected it to be given to him.

No.

Fuck that.

Natalie - the nurse - came through for me. She managed to get hold of my mum who came and picked me up. I never told her what happened. The memory has only just popped back to me now, about what landed me in hospital, and I couldn't say for definite whether it was there after I had woken up in the bed or whether I am only just remembering it again for the first time now. Hard to tell. My memories are so confused; all over the place with them. For all I know - I woke up in hospital and didn't recall the reasons for being there until now. Unlikely but possible.

Dad didn't come to see me. He didn't even phone. He avoided me. At least now I know why. Knowing I couldn't remember how I got there, he probably didn't want to show up on the off-chance it jogged my memory. He didn't even let me stay at their house for a while. I was told I shouldn't be alone for twenty-four hours and mum said she'd look after me. She had to come round my tiny flat to do so. Well he doesn't have a choice but to let me in now. I need to stay with them. I need some sanctuary whilst I try and get over what I've been through… Forget the taste of flesh I've grown accustomed to.

Can't put it off any longer. Need to get out of the open. Need to lock myself away.

I opened the car door and stormed towards mum and dad's house. The door opened just as I got there; dad was on his way to work. He jumped at the sight of me. Do I look that frightful?

"What are you doing here?" he hissed.

So much hostility. I'm trying to think back, trying to remember, whether I knew he was fucking about behind mum's back before our confrontation which landed me in the hospital. More to the point, did dad know he'd been spotted? It would explain why he hated me so much and was determined to get me away from the house. Or am I just putting things into place myself, finding excuses and reasons as to why he's such an asshole to me? Need to stop trying to figure out the past and concentrate on the future. It's doing me nothing but giving me a stinking headache; unless that's down to withdrawal symptoms from the lack of drugs in the water I'd been drinking?

"I need to talk to you," I said.

He stepped out of the house and closed the door before mum heard me.

"We had an agreement," he said.

He started to walk towards his car, keys in hand. I called out to him and told him to turn around. He did and immediately spotted the gun in my hand.

"We need to go in the house now," I told him.

"What the hell are you doing?" he asked.

The front door opened - making me jump - and mum appeared, "You forgot..." she stopped dead when she saw me standing there. I'm not sure whether she was surprised to see me or whether she was surprised to see the gun. "What's going on?" she asked.

"I need to talk to you both. Please."

Dad looked at mum. She backed away from the door, holding it open for me. I didn't wait for a verbal invitation and stepped into the house, closely followed by dad. He closed the door behind him. Mum led me through to the living room.

"What's happened?" she asked. "Why have you got a gun? You look terrible... What has been going on? I've been trying to call you for days now, even went by the flat! Where have you been?"

"Just sit down!" I shouted. A shout which made mum jump, and even took me by surprise.

"Put the fucking gun down!" dad hissed. "You're scaring your mother!"

"Honey - what's happened to you? Where have you been?"

Mum sat down on the sofa. I turned to dad and stared at him until he too joined her on the sofa. I didn't sit. I stood by the fireplace unsure of where to start. Wherever I chose the starting point to be, I knew it would sound far -fetched.

"Please talk to us," mum said.

"Okay. Okay." I turned to dad. "My memory isn't what is used to be," I told him. He didn't respond. "I was wondering whether you could help me out a bit," I continued.

Mum looked at dad as though trying to urge him to respond.

"I remember seeing you with that woman," I went on, "I remember seeing you kissing her but I can't remember whether you were always an asshole to me or whether you became such when you found out I knew about your affair…"

Mum continued looking at dad. The devastation clear on her face.

"What's this?" she asked him.

"I don't know what you're talking about," dad said, his face red.

"You do though." I turned to mum, "Do you remember when you came to get me at the hospital? I had an accident but no one really knew what happened… Well, dad knew. Dad caused it."

He turned to mum, "I don't know what he is talking about."

"You do though. We were talking, I confronted you about it, you shoved me, I hit my head on the wall and was knocked out. I'm guessing you phoned the ambulance before disappearing? Is that right? I mean you clearly didn't come with me. Had you come… We wouldn't have had to phone mum. I wouldn't have woken up in the hospital bed alone…"

"Is this true?" mum no longer looked devastated. She looked disgusted.

"So my original question - to help clear up my memories - was there ever a time when you loved me or have you always hated me? And was there a time when you loved mum or have you always cheated on her? I just think - if I am to get over what has been happening to me these past few days - I need to get things straight in my head."

"I don't know what you have been doing these past few days, I don't know where you have been - or what you have been smoking - but… Whatever you think you know... You're clearly mixed up. Perhaps you should lay off watching movies and television shows?" dad said. His voice was low, almost threatening. I wasn't worried. I wasn't even slightly concerned. I had been to places he couldn't even comprehend and - despite wanting to move on with my life - I was more than happy to give him a first glance taste of what I'd been through.

"I'll tell you where I have been," I said before explaining all that I had been through since waking up in that godforsaken shit-hole of a compound. The confusion, the fake family, the end of the world, the hunger... They looked shocked and that was even before I told them about the man I'd killed. The man I'd eaten... And the other people we'd eaten. By the time I got to the end of the story - the truth about it being an experiment that I had inadvertently signed up for - I was sure they'd given up listening completely; too stunned by my murderous admissions. "Well?" I said. "Say something..."

No one said anything. They just sat there, staring at me - a look of utter disbelief on their faces. A hint of disgust and shame mixed in.

"Are you on drugs? Is that where you've been these past couple of days? Some dirty drug den? Been sitting there with some new friends, getting off your face and making up stories?" said dad. "Is that where you plucked the alleged affair from? And the violent attack I supposedly subjected you to?"

"Fuck you," I spat back at him.

Mum didn't say anything. It was clear she'd had a massive overload of information to deal with and was struggling to process it all. I don't blame her. Had the shoe been on the other foot, I would have struggled too.

"Where have you been?" mum asked. "Really? Where have you been? I've been worried about you."

I turned to dad, "Were you worried about me?"

He didn't answer. He didn't have to. If he felt anything - it would be disappointment that I reappeared back on the scene again.

I asked him again, "Were you ever worried about me?"

"I want you out of my house," he said.

"Answer the question!" I shouted. "Were you ever worried about me?!"

"No!" he shouted back. "No, I wasn't!"

Mum burst into tears as she realised her family was beyond repair. No coming back from this.

Dad continued, "I wasn't worried about you in the slightest."

"Well you should have been!"

I raised the gun up to his head and pulled the trigger. It clicked. Nothing else. No bullets, no bang, nothing. Empty? Fuck. Still - didn't stop both him and mum from visibly jumping as they both feared the worst. Fine - he should have feared the worst... The gun was aimed at him but what was mum worried about? I was trying to set her free. I was trying to rid her of the one thing in her life truly holding her back from being the great person she could have been.

Dad started laughing, "Very good. You got me. Now get the fuck out of my house and don't you dare darken my doorstep again. You hear me?"

I dropped the gun and smiled.

"Okay," I said.

He stood up and walked towards the living room door, as though leading me back through to the front door.

"Before I go," I said, "I'm hungry... Do you mind if I at least get something for the road?" I looked at mum because I knew she wouldn't be able to say no to me. She had never been able to say no to me. She nodded and I smiled. She was always there for me. No matter what I did.

I walked towards the doorway to the hall. Dad was standing there. I stopped in front of him. He looked at me, confused why I wasn't grabbing something from the kitchen so I could be on my merry way.

"Just grab a packet of crisps - hell, include a chocolate biscuit with that if you want - and leave. Enough is enough. We don't want you around here anymore."

I grabbed him by his ears and pulled him towards me. Everything happened so fast he didn't fight back as I sunk my teeth into him. He screamed as I ripped a piece of nose and lip from his face. Mum screamed too as I sunk my teeth into dad again; this time tearing out his throat - adam's apple and all. He started to choke and gargle but I wasn't done with him. I bit him again and again, each time tearing more flesh from bone. Each little piece, I swallowed as the meat cured me of my hunger. Mum was screaming for me to get off him but still I ignored her.

I let go of him and he dropped onto his knees with his hands at his throat, trying to stem the flow of blood (not happening). He wasn't suffering enough, though. I needed him to suffer more. I put one hand behind his head, to steady him, and pushed two fingers and my thumb into his eye-socket; two fingers above and the thumb below, allowing me to get a good grip of his eyeball. I ripped it from his head and popped it straight into my mouth. I bit down hard and felt it squish between my teeth; lovely juices filling my mouth as I wondered whether he was able to see any of this still. They say a heart can continue beating once it has been removed from a chest cavity... Well... Can an eye see for a while longer if that too has been removed. Can it see itself getting swallowed into the digestive system. Dad didn't scream. He was too far gone; still gargling on his own blood, choking as he deserved to. I let go of him and he dropped to the floor. His gargles becoming less frequent. I turned to mum and immediately felt a rush of guilt...

"Sorry, did you want some?" I asked.

I walked over to her and she flinched away. I froze. What? She thought I was going to hurt her? Of course I wasn't going to hurt her. Why would she think such a thing? I love her. She's always been there for me and now I'll always be there for her.

"I need you," I told her.

I sat down next to her and turned my body to face her. I put my hands on her hands (which were on her lap) and tried my best to reassure her that everything was going to be okay.

"I need you to help me, just as I'll help you. You know, so we can both move forward from this. The government people - the ones who put me in that fucking test... They might come for me so I can't go home. I created a distraction to help me get away and hopefully they'll forget about me but... I need you to help hide me. And - although I don't know how - I need you to help me move on and forget about all the bad things I've done..."

Mum didn't say anything nor did she look very good. Her face was pale. She was shaking. Was she going into shock? She can't be. I've set her free. She should be happy. She should be as happy as I am for getting home to her.

"Are you okay?" I asked. "I realise this is a lot to take in." I pointed over to dad, "Did you want something to eat? A bit of energy to help you cope and think straight?" She still didn't reply to me; just sat there shaking. I felt myself getting angry at her. No. Not angry. I was getting frustrated. "Mum! Talk to me! I've gone through hell to get back to you!" I lifted my hand out of frustration. I wasn't going to do anything - it was more of an involuntary movement.

"Don't hurt me!" mum flinched away from me.

"What?" I was shocked by her outburst. "I'm not doing to hurt you!" I reached across to her and pulled her close to me, putting my arms around her. "I'm not going to hurt you… I love you!"

She was still crying, "I love you too…" she said.

I pulled away from her, "You do? Even after everything I've told you?"

She nodded. Was she just saying this because she thought I wanted to hear it? No. She couldn't have been. She does love me. It's obvious she loves me; all that she has done for me over the years. Of course she loves me. I leaned forward to her and kissed her. I paused. I pulled away slightly and stared into her eyes. She does love me.

"What?" she asked.

She wiped a tear from cheek. Still looked fearful. We can turn this around though. I used to do this with my girlfriend, before she left me. We'd have a little argument and then we'd make up… I leaned forward and kissed mum again, sliding my tongue into her mouth. I felt her body tense in my grip. It's fine. She'll relax into it. I know she will. Just like Mother and Sister did, she'll enjoy it. I held her close as I continued to explore the inside of her mouth with my tongue; caressing her own tongue as I did so. I moved my hand down to her breast and gave it a gentle squeeze. I do love her. I've always loved her, just as she has always loved me. My hand moved from breast down, between her legs. She flinched at my touch but it's okay. It's still okay. She'll settle into it once I warm her up. She'll enjoy it. I'll make sure she does. I need her to. I want to taste her cum when I lick at her pussy. I need to taste it…

I've always wanted to taste it.

And - what - it took the experiment to make me realise this?

What am I doing? Of course it didn't take the experiment to make me realise it. It's just changed the way I think. I pulled away from mum. She breathed out heavily (relief?) and stood up she started to walk towards the door only to stop close to dad's body. Hard to judge what was going through her mind. Was she going to have a taste?

"What are you doing?" I asked.

She hesitated, "I - er - I... I was going to get a drink."

No. I don't agree with that - the experiment changing me. I've always wanted this. Mum has always wanted this. Looking at our situation now, the way she helped me as I grew up - it's obvious now. It's crystal fucking clear. I jumped up from the sofa and hurried over to mum. I put my hands on her shoulder (she flinched) and span her around so that she was facing me. Hands moved to arse as I pressed my erection against her before sliding my tongue back into her mouth. She feels tense again. She'll relax. We just need to get comfortable. Probably move things away from The Snack. I'm used to this but she isn't. I shouldn't expect her to settle into fucking in front of dead folk as easily as I can now.

"Follow me," I took her hand and pulled her from the room. I lead her up the stairs towards the room she once stared with the Fillet Steak.

"I thought you were hungry?" mum said. "Why don't you go and have a wash and I'll prepare you a nice sandwich. How does that sound? Or a fry-up? I have bacon..." she sounded nervous. Why does she so nervous? She knows she wants this as much as I do.

I pulled her into the room and pushed her back on the bed, telling her to relax. She froze when she saw the knife tucked between belt and trouser.

"I'll tell you, that has got me out of some sticky situations," I joked. I pulled it from where it rested and threw it to the floor. "Now, where were we?"

I climbed on top of mum and continued to kiss her passionately. She squirmed underneath me - clearly getting into things.

EPILOGUE

True Love and Rotting Dead F*cks

All day I had fucked mum. To my surprise, she liked it rough. To my surprise, she was a screamer - really getting into it as I continually hit her sweet spot with moves taught to me by Mother and Sister. Because I was self-conscious about her having at least one orgasm I ensured I edged myself to begin with so I could continually pound her whilst reaching down and stroking her clitoris. I'd get myself right to the point of orgasm and stop for a second or two. I'd carry on and get to the point of happiness and - again - I'd stop. Only when I knew for sure that she'd cum... Only then did I really let myself go, and on more than one occasion (by choice). I didn't want to stop fucking her, even after my first ejaculation. The sweet tingling, the twitching cock as I fired stream after stream of hot, sticky spunk into her warm, inviting cunt. As soon as I'd shot my load, I ensured I carried on despite the sensitivity. Once you get past the first couple of minutes... Everything becomes numb and you can soon get back into the swing of pumping away - with little discomfort - until you fire off another load.

I rolled from her body between the second and third orgasm. I wanted to reach the third - the one I wanted to fire down her throat - but couldn't quite get there. So hungry, so tired... hardly surprising after everything I'd been through and the lack of sleep I'd had. I jumped up and walked through to the bathroom, before coming back with a towel. I threw it to mum who was curled into a little ball and still shaking. Lucky cow still in the throes of an orgasm. I must have hit the spot just right. She'll be bragging about that to her friends over coffee within a week, or two. I laughed at the thought.

"You okay?" I asked.

She didn't say anything. Clearly tired her out.

"Can I get you anything? A drink? Piece of fillet steak?"

Again, she didn't say anything. I shrugged it off and put it down to how tired she must be. She's getting on a bit now. Clearly I'd taken it out of her a bit. Probably isn't used to marathon sessions like that. Not with dad anyway. I sat on the edge of the bed and reached over to the television control sitting on the bedside cabinet. A press of the red button and the television - in the corner of the room - flickered into life. The News.

"Funny - I don't think I missed the television at all when I was out in the woods," I said.

Mum didn't say anything. I turned my head to see if she had heard me. She was crying.

"Don't worry. I'm home now. I'm safe."

Sweet of her to worry about me so. I honestly think we're about to embark on a really special relationship together. Considering everything I've gone through, everything that has happened - it really is quite exciting. I patted her on the bum and told her to rest up so we can carry on where we left off... I want to hit that third orgasm. I turned my attention back to the television. Helicopter footage played on the screen - over some woods. A series of cabins. I knew exactly what it was. Where it was. The compound. Some of the cabins were on fire. I turned the television up and a reporter spoke of explosions and rioting down below. What the hell happened? Was this part of the distraction I caused? Had things got truly out of hand? I continued to watch the report. On screen you could clearly see people heading into the woods. I couldn't help but laugh - proud that I caused this - before wondering whether these people were infected or whether they were soldiers running from a situation they couldn't control. Whatever the scenario, I don't care. Fuck them. They got what they deserved. Mum moved on the bed behind me.

"You okay?" I asked.

Probably using the towel to clean herself up a bit. Could have answered me though. I turned towards her and was shocked to see she had my knife in her shaking hand. Tears streaming down her face, blade pointed right at me.

I asked again, "You okay?"

THE END

Manufactured by Amazon.ca
Bolton, ON